As we are about to get a taxi, a Rolls pulls up. It's the young man who poured the beer on the other fellow's head.

'Hello,' he says, 'want a lift home?'

It's not my usual custom to accept lifts from strange men, but then these are unusual circumstances. We jump in. He introduces himself.

'I'm Jake von Cartnoy.'

He sits back expectantly as we swish down the road. Kate and I haven't the faintest idea who he is, but then, as I explain, we have been out of the country a lot recently. Never mind out of the country, Kate is practically out of her T-shirt as she introduces herself.

'How would you like some dinner? That dancing looked very energetic. We can always pop in at Carrier's for a snack.' . . .

Carrier's proves to be even better than I had imagined, and Jake is a marvellous host. It turns out he directs TV commercials, which sounds like a wonderful way of earning a living . . .

Kate likes him too. Not one of these situations again, I find myself hoping. Not one of these situations with attractive rich bastards. As I sip my third brandy I find myself praying we don't get into anything complicated again like last time . . .

D1464774

Also by Penny Sutton

THE JUMBO JET GIRLS

Penny Sutton

I'm Penny, Fly Me

Futura Publications Limited

A Futura Book

First published in Great Britain in 1975
by Futura Publications Limited

Copyright © Justin Cartwright and
Christopher Wood 1975

This book is sold subject to the condition
that it shall not, by way of trade or
otherwise, be lent, re-sold, hired out or
otherwise circulated without the publisher's
prior consent in any form of binding or
cover other than that in which it is
published and without a similar condition
including this condition being imposed on the
subsequent purchaser

ISBN 0 8600 7216 9

Printed in Great Britain by
Cox & Wyman Ltd,
London, Reading and Fakenham

Futura Publications Limited
49 Poland Street, London W1A 2LG

CHAPTER ONE

'When you've burnt all your boats, you've got to learn to swim,' says my old friend and colleague, Kate Goodbody. She's given to a bit of philosophy now and then. Actually, what she means is quite simple. After our experiences in America (see *The Jumbo Jet Girls* by Penny Sutton) we returned to London, sadder, but, alas, no wiser. After a while we find ourselves penniless, jobless and bored. Not only that, but we have no hope of getting back into the regular airline business after my publicity. So it is swim or sink.

At the moment we are sinking. We've sunk so far that we've taken up go-go dancing. It's good for the figure, so I keep telling myself, and after five lessons, says Maurice, our amiable coach, we'll be able to dance at Covent Garden.

'Covent Garden in a pair of thigh boots and a tasselled bikini,' snorts Kate, 'you must be joking.'

'Sure, the Coach and Horses, Covent Garden.'

'You are a one, Morrie, now get your hands off,' I say.

Maurice is not a big man, about fifty, who runs his go-go dancing school from a flat in Soho so small you couldn't swing a Manx cat in it. He has progressed through ten vocations to this peak as a go-go instructor and agent, including a spell as a freelance lorry unloader. Trouble was, as he explains it, they weren't his lorries and some geezer caught him at it. So when he came out he decided to go straight, at least till something better came along.

'Obviously didn't get much in the nick, did you Maurice,' says Kate as she detaches his hand from her right

5

buttock, where he has thoughtfully placed it to guide her through a difficult routine, involving shaking your hips and your bust in different directions. Maurice actually makes his money, as he later confides to us, in supplying costumes and procuring jobs for the graduates of the Maurice Bussmann dance school of Old Compton Street. Still, he's not a bad sort and five lessons for ten quid seems reasonable.

After the first day, Kate and I feel like hell. We are stiff all over.

'Sex is no substitute for exercise,' says she.

'I don't know, I mean I never feel stiff like this.'

'That's just the point. If you want to make the big time you have to be dedicated. No sex before away matches.'

Poor Kate, I think she is losing her marbles since she met that football player, but I don't like to say anything.

We don our leotards. ('Essential part of the game girls, to you a knock-down price, four pounds and fifty pence') and Maurice puts on a record, something by Ike and Tina Turner. He watches Kate trying to compress her bouncy frame into a tiny leotard with interest.

'Take off a few pounds, and you'll be a winner, kid.' I think Morrie has been watching 'A Star is Born' on telly. He's smoking a long cigar and he's very expansive. Fortunately so are our leotards and we manage to get into them in the end, with a little unnecessary help from Maurice.

'Now line up – right a-one, a-two, a-one two three, arms up, and down a-one two a-three, stick them out Penny, that's what the customers are paying for. That's good, that's terrific.'

Perhaps he's referring to the fact that my leotard is slipping off my shoulders.

'Don't stop, good, together now, contraction, a-one two, one two, now turn – great.'

By the end of Ike and Tina Turner we are completely shagged-out.

'You've got to be able to dance to ten records in an evening, non-stop. Now come on, let's do a really slow, sexy number, and smile, like you're having a great time.'

I have to hand it to Maurice, he's full of enthusiasm. We contract, gyrate, bend, wiggle and dance till we've got blisters. Funny thing is, we feel like stars in no time. Maurice is very persuasive.

'They'll love you girls at the Star and Garter. You're going to knock them dead at the Black Bull.' If Kate's bra snaps again, that could literally be true. Morrie helps scoop her back into her leotard. Very helpful fellow, Mr Bussmann, and it's nice to see someone who enjoys his work so.

'Couple more lessons and I'll have you on the road. After the first time it's easy. You would make a fortune topless, you know,' he says eyeing us, 'want to try?'

'No thanks.'

'Pity, pity. Such talent going to waste. Never mind let's go. One, two, three.'

And so it goes on. By the fifth day, we're pretty good, though I don't suppose Pan's People are getting worried. Morrie has booked us for our first performance at a pub in Islington, £10 each for the night, dancing for one hour in two spells. Unfortunately, we have to buy our costumes, from Maurice, if we want the job.

'I suggest gold lamé pants and these long gold boots here, plus the top, let me see, I can let you have the lot for £25.'

I try on the boots and then the pants. They are so small I think he must have got them from a brownie surplus sale and dyed them gold.

'No, no. That's right. They're terrific. Let's see the top.'

I try this on. It is a push-up bra in gold lamé which just about covers my nipples, when I am standing up straight.

It makes my cleavage so pronounced I could almost keep my sandwiches down there. Still, as Maurice so wisely points out, that's show business. Kate has the same problem only bigger if you know what I mean. I don't have much confidence in this clobber, but a few minutes of our routine and they don't actually disintegrate, so I am a bit happier. The trouble is, it's one thing doing all this in front of Maurice, but what about all those louts with a glass of beer in their hands, I ask myself nervously? Kate has fallen a bit silent too, which is very ominous. Because all of a sudden as we stand there almost naked, boobs dished up like two creme caramels, or four really, and see ourselves in the mirror, we realize what we're in for.

'Don't worry,' says Maurice.

But we do.

Friday is our big night, and we are worried stiff. Morrie is all confidence, but I guess that by the time he has got the booking and sold us the clothes, he could not care less. And I guess right. When we turn up at the pub in question, there is no sign of our trainer. The publican, Fred, shows us to a tiny room upstairs and tells us to get ready in ten minutes. I am just doing up my bra, and Kate has only her pants on when Fred makes an unscheduled entrance. Kate and I are getting used to show business by now so we pretend this happens every day.

'You can't wear that.' Fred is looking at my bra.

'What do you mean?'

'This is topless go-go dancing.'

'Topless, are you serious?'

'Course I'm bloody serious, this pub would get a bad name if you came down in them corsets.'

'Look, Mr Fred, it may be OK for girls with thirty-two inch busts to bounce about out there for half an hour, but Kate and I are in another league.'

'Yes, well, see what you mean. Hold on. Don't go away.'

He hurries off. Kate and I begin to laugh. That's the good thing about Kate, you can't be serious with her for long. The situation is terrible. From below in the pub, we hear that the natives are getting restless.

'We want the Goldies,' they are crying between bouts of drinking. Morrie, now unhappily unable to be with us, has billed us as the Goldies. Very inventive man, Morrie.

Fred comes back. 'Here, put these on.'

These are sort of slings with two bits of thong which go round the neck and encircle each boob.

'I'll wear that on two conditions. One – you get me a double whisky now. And two, you pay us £20 each for the night.'

'Hear, hear,' I chip in.

Actually we are holding all the cards, it turns out, because downstairs it sounds as though the place is beginning to break up. Perhaps it is the McAlpine office party. I am almost hysterical as I put the sling on. It does offer some support, but it leaves me absolutely naked on top. My only consolation is that I don't know anybody who lives in Islington. Or do I?

Fred gives us each a large whisky, races downstairs, and after a moment an expectant hush falls on the waiting yobbos.

'One, two, three four, testing, testing.' The microphone emits some banshee wails. He blows in it.

'And now ladies and gentlemen, fresh from their triumph in Paris, the fabulous Goldies.' With some difficulty he puts on a record and we stride in.

All we can see is a mass of faces and beer glasses, all staring, it seems to me at my boobs. If boobs could blush, mine would be crimson.

'A-one, a-two, a-one two three,' says Kate, and off we go.

9

At first we are a little stiff, but I think there is a bit of the exhibitionist in all girls; as Kate once said, if you've got it, flaunt it, and we really get going. The yobbos are ecstatic. One is so ecstatic that he tries to get on the platform with us, but Fred's helpers soon put him back where he belongs. The record changes to something a bit slower, Kate and I face each other and do one of the routines Morrie has taught us. It drives the crowd wild. It's not surprising, because the platform is only the size of a large dining room table, and Kate and I are practically dancing cheek to cheek. Kate, is loving it and I am beginning to relax. We bump and grind like a pair of seasoned strippers. A couple of fast numbers and we are off. The crowd in the bar get right back to their drinking. We are exhausted, mainly from the tension, but Fred assures us we were terrific.

'This is a hell of a long way from being stewardesses,' says Kate, who can sometimes state the obvious.

We have one unfortunate incident later in the evening on our second appearance. It is getting a bit late and the patrons are becoming louder and rowdier. I am terrified the whole lot are suddenly going to rush the stage and tear us to pieces. Still, we go on leaping about when suddenly one man makes a grab for Kate's pants. She gives a little feint that Georgie Best would be proud of, but her pursuer slips and his pint goes all over a quiet, good-looking young man in the front row. When he has wiped the beer off his Rayban glasses, he stands up empties his pint on the other bloke's head, and calmly walks out of the pub. We are so stunned, we stop dancing. Fred calls Time and gestures for us to get off stage. We don't need another invitation because tempers in the pub are getting a little heated.

In fact by the time we are changed and ready to go home, the pub is in an uproar. The police around here are obviously used to this sort of thing, because they move in like the wrath of God. We are quite frightened by the tables flying about and the crunch of beer glasses on the pavement. Fred looks as though he wishes he had become a poultry sexer instead of a publican, shakes his head sadly as he gives us our money.

'That's me licence for go-go dancing gone. I'm too soft for this game. Still, you was terrific. If the beaks don't take it away by next week, I'll get in touch with Maurice and you can come back.'

We feel a little sorry for him as he stands there in the wreckage of his pub. Even the plastic flowers have wilted and you could practically surf on the beer that's lying around. Still £20 is welcome, and we both agree that go-go dancing is exciting. As we are about to get a taxi, a Rolls pulls up. It's the young man who poured the beer on the other fellow's head.

'Hello,' he says, 'want a lift home?'

It's not my usual custom to accept lifts from strange men, but then these are unusual circumstances. We jump in. He introduces himself.

'I'm Jake von Cartnoy.'

He sits back expectantly as we swish down the road. Kate and I haven't the faintest idea who he is, but then as I explain, we have been out of the country a lot recently. Never mind out of the country, Kate is practically out of her T-shirt as she introduces herself.

'How would you like some dinner? That dancing looked very energetic. We can always pop in at Carrier's for a snack.'

It's a pick-up, but then a pick-up in a Rolls and dinner at Carrier's is something else. Jake says that Bob will always find him a table.

Carrier's proves to be even better than I had imagined, and Jake is a marvellous host. It turns out he directs TV commercials, which sounds like a wonderful way of earning a living. Judging by the bill, which I catch a glimpse of, it has to be. He has told us all about filming in Jamaica and all the other exotic places he goes. Much to my surprise I find I really quite like him, and not just because he is rich and has a Rolls. There is some vitality in him that you don't get in your run of the mill accountants and that sort. Jake has had a hard boyhood in East Ham, and come up through the world of advertising to his present position of eminence. But when he explains it all to us, it is with a sense of humour, like when he got his first Rolls, he pulled up at a garage for petrol and the attendant said: 'You chauffeurs get all the luck.'

Kate likes him too. Not one of these situations again, I find myself hoping. Not one of these situations with attractive, rich, bastards. As I sip my third brandy I find myself praying we don't get into anything complicated again like last time.

My prayers are not answered. Alas!

CHAPTER TWO

Over the next few weeks Kate and I expose ourselves all over London. It soon becomes as natural as anything to dance about near naked with fifty leering men standing by. We pop out in Streatham, Hampstead, and even Mayfair. Only once do we run into someone we once knew, a pilot, but he isn't going to say anything because the girl he is with is not nearly as closely related to him as his wife. Yes, we become a wonderful pair of troupers, and make a few bob into the bargain. Maurice, for all his tricks, proves to be a good agent. But it is a million miles away from airline work, which is what we know.

Jake and I are becoming firm friends. Trouble is, so are Jake and Kate. And firm is the operative word, I am afraid. As Jake says, he likes us both so much, how could he possibly choose? We both have a soft spot for this type of self-confident bastard. As we are out three nights a week and some lunch hours go-go dancing, it doesn't leave much time for Jake, so we decide to give him a night each week until we can come to a more suitable arrangement. To-night, still a bit weak from a rough lunchtime session at the Blue Boar in Hammersmith, I am going with Jake to a preview of a film made by one of his friends. It's called 'Sex in the Vicarage' but as Jake explains it, his friend has a strong ecclesiastical bent, and who am I to argue?

The film itself is pretty dire, but they all say it will do well in the provinces, wherever they are, but really the confessions of a vicar and his goings-on with the girls in the choir, all set in a Norfolk vicarage, is not my scene. Jake especially likes the bit where the vicar is doffing his robes and a girl comes in and asks if she can play the organ. He replies, 'Many are called, but few are chosen.' At least he would have said that if the picture and the words had been more or less synchronized. As Jake explains to me, it's just a first cut.

After the film we all go off to a marvellous house in Richmond for a party. The place is full of models, young hopefuls all, long-haired young men who do things with the camera, slightly drunken film critics, who seem keener to get to grips with the starlets than the intellectual challenge of the film, and even a famous director or two. Everyone knows Jake, and he introduces me around freely. After a few champagne cocktails, I am beginning to put the horrors of the Blue Boar right out of my mind.

Jake introduces me to a film producer in advertising and we fall into conversation while he is off being charming to everybody.

'What do you do?'

'Well at the moment, I am a go-go dancer.' As his eyes begin to light up like a child's at the sight of an ice cream, I hasten to add, 'but really I am an airline stewardess. It's just that I have blotted my copybook a bit with the big airlines.'

I don't know why, but he's a good listener, and I tell him the whole story.

'Look, give me your number, I might have something for you and your friend.'

We have a dance and I think no more of it, particularly as David, as he's called, is holding me very, very tight. Before he can actually imprint his body on me, Jake comes and rescues me.

'Piss off and grope somebody else's bird,' he says good-humouredly.

David seems to think it's quite funny too, and there are

no hard feelings, though nobody consults me. Still compared with go-go dancing, this is positively refined.

'Very important cat that,' says Jake, 'biggest producer in the business, handles about two hundred commercials a year. You can believe most of what he says, which is more than you can for the others. Always on about the bloody Bahamas, but in the end you get as far as Camber Sands with a few palm trees dressed in. And don't believe the nonsense about come round tomorrow and meet someone important and he'll get you in commercials if you're nice to him.'

Forearmed is forewarned, and I get a lot of this line of dialogue in the course of the evening. In my experience, film and photographic parties are always the wildest things going, I suppose because of the amount of pretty young girls in the business. This one begins to deteriorate fast, and by the time Jake and I get ready to leave it is getting out of hand. It would do credit to a brothel in Marseilles. I am a bit intrigued to see what's going on, particularly as I hear some funny noises from a dark room up the stairs, but Jake tells me they are showing the out-takes of the film, that is the bits they couldn't use either because they were too blue or something went wrong. He is very cool about it so we leave.

It is the first time he has taken me home to his flat in Covent Garden. It's an old warehouse converted as a film studio on two floors and a fantastic flat on the top floor, keeping all the old beams and even some of the winding machinery.

'What's that for,' I ask, all wide-eyed innocence, 'an instrument of torture?'

'Yes for girls who don't do what I say. I attach their hands to that end and their feet to the other and turn the handle. They soon give in.'

'Anything but not the rack,' I plead.

'Anything?'

'Well, almost.'

'OK. There's one small thing you can do for me if you are to be saved.'

'What's that?'

'Scrub my back in the bath.'

'Oh my goodness, that's naughty.'

He runs the bath, which is a giant size, practically big enough to convert into a dolphinarium and slips out of his cord suit and lace shirt in a flash. This is obviously not a new routine for him, even the lights in the bathroom are on dimmers, but I take the plunge, so to speak. I am glad I have put on a sexy black, uplift bra, because all men I know find them mind-blowing. Extraordinary. As I slip it off, my back turned towards him, I get the feeling something is stirring down in the depths there. I just keep my panties on as I begin to scrub his back. I can't seem to keep my hands from wandering further afield, however.

'That's not my back,' he complains.

'Oh, I am sorry. Perhaps this is your back. Here, what's this?'

'That's my loofah. I never go anywhere without it.'

He grabs me and pulls me into the bath with him, panties and all. We giggle and tickle each other. He loves soaping my breasts, and I must say I feel in terrific shape after all that go-go dancing. My stomach is lean and flat as it hasn't been since I was a budding thirteen-year-old gymnast at school. Alas, boys came along and diverted my energies, but that's another story.

Well this sort of thing can't go on for long and it doesn't. Still wet we find ourselves on the fleecy rug by the bath. There is something terribly sexy about wet, soapy bodies. I take only a few seconds to get my sodden panties off and he takes even less time to get on top of me. We are so wet and soapy that I am afraid he may slip off, but we find a way of anchoring ourselves together. He begins to move inside me and I come almost immediately. By the time it is over we have skated all around the bathroom floor. I must say, I think sex should not be too solemn, and this certainly isn't, but I am a little disturbed by the practised ease with which he goes about the whole thing. I mean, supposing he and Kate had been up to this the night before? I try not to think about it as we sip a drink, me wearing one of his dressing gowns, and listen to his fantastic stereo. It is a bad sign for me when I begin to get jealous – it usually means that love is rearing its ugly head, and I've hardly got over my terrible experience of seeing someone I loved killed before my eyes. (See *The Jumbo Jet Girls* by Penny Sutton.) I can understand why Kate likes him too, he's so easy to get on with and so easy to talk to, even though he does not give much away himself.

Eventually we go to bed and I sleep with my arms around him most of the night. Some men don't like being touched as they sleep, but I find all the ones I really like love sleeping curled up together. It has other advantages too. I wake up and find him already making love to me more than once during the night, which is better than a slap in the face with a wet fish, as they say.

The telephone rings at some ungodly hour; Jake's assistant.

'Look, go away, I told you not to call before 11.00. What? Oh, OK, I'll get up.'

He gets up.

'Make us some breakfast, there's a dear, I've got to ring old Dave, the one from the party, about a job. My lad says it's a very big one.'

As I make some scrambled eggs and bacon, I hear him muttering on the phone. After a while he comes rushing in.

'Jesus, darling, this is fantastic. Dave is giving me the

British American airline job to do. And he wants you to be in it, with Kate.'

This is like Hughie Green gone mad. Me? What for? It turns out they are not allowed to use models in commercials any more so they have to use actresses, who by and large aren't pretty enough, or real stewardesses. Equity. Dave thinks it would be a great idea if we played the part of the stewardesses. It's not decided yet, but he thinks he can swing it. Even Jake is excited.

'This is the best job of the year for me. Hundreds of locations, free travel from the airline and no expense spared to get the right stuff. You are fantastic.' As usual I don't bother to ask about money or anything like that. I am so delighted to get into something to do with airlines again – I mean Islington on a rainy Sunday morning twirling your tassels is a far cry from Nassau, isn't it?

Kate is suspicious. 'Remember that bastard Richard and the nude photography?'

She dampens my enthusiasm for a while, but we agree it's worth having a good hard look at it before we turn it down. I have a theory, learned the hard way, that nothing is quite as good as it seems to be at first, with a few notable exceptions we won't go into here. But once the machine begins to roll, Kate and I are helpless. That very afternoon we are told to come for an interview at an advertising agency, and they are going to pick the girls for the job.

Although I must be the cleanest girl in London after my experiences of the previous night, I am feeling a little jaded, so Kate and I rush off to a nearby beauty salon and get our faces and hair done by experts. Not only experts, but highway robbers – it costs us £15 each.

'Penny, I hope this isn't one of your terrible girl-guide mistakes.'

'Think of it as an investment, dear.'

'In what?'

'In the old firm of Goodbody and Sutton.'

'Who would want to give up a steady job, lots of prospects, pension fund, luncheon vouchers as a freelance go-go dancer for the uncertainties of the film world?'

'Me.'

'And me.'

'It's settled then. Well, if they still want us.'

The advertising agency is a large building on a smart square in SW1. It's all chrome and glass and bright young men in suits dashing about looking purposeful.

When the receptionist looks up from her nail varnishing, we tell her we've come about British American Airways.

'Sixth floor, first door on your left. They'll come for you there.' She goes back to her nails with a barely concealed boredom.

'Oh by the way,' says Kate as we are going to the lift.

'Yes dear?' says the receptionist wearily.

'That green nail polish doesn't go with your red nose.'

Mercifully the lift door opens and we rush inside, colliding with the tea lady, who gives a disdainful snort and wheels her trolley out. In their Take 6 suits and regulation short-long hair the men who pile in after us look like trainee Homepride Flour Graders. One of them tries a feeble chat-up in the lift but we have other, bigger things on our mind. And I am not talking about Jake's loofah.

We wait in a large room, with a screen and lots of low, slinky chairs to see what is going to happen. Initially, nothing. Kate and I begin to get a bit bored, but we don't think we can really just leave. We have been told to bring bikinis along in case they want to see our figures, funny that, even if you were doing a film about dog food, they would want to see you in the altogether. Maybe it's something to do with the job – they feel models and people like that are in their power. Anyway, after baring all in some of the seediest pubs in London, Kate and I aren't too worried about stripping off. I decide to try on my new bikini, bought especially for the occasion. Kate shuts the door and locks it. My new bikini is French, of soft knitted material, which just about covers what is necessary. Just as I am taking off my skirt, a voice comes over a loudspeaker.

'Good afternoon, this is David Stanstead here, could you girls get into your bikinis and we will be along in a few minutes.'

'All right,' I say, addressing the speaker rather foolishly.

We have some difficulty getting me into my bikini. Kate has to do some running repairs on the strap at the back, which is threatening to go at any moment.

'It will be OK if you don't breathe.'

'Thanks. You're a pal. Yours will be OK if you have breast surgery.'

'Don't be disgusting. Uggh. What a grubby little mind.'

Kate has always been spectacular in a bikini, being rather slim all over except at the front; sometimes when I am being unkind I think they got two girls mixed up, one tall thin one and one large buxom one. Still it's a combination that seems to work.

We stand around in our bikinis admiring ourselves for a few more minutes, when there comes a knock on the door. We let David Stanstead in and a small tribe of other people, most of them carrying pads and folders and looking very concerned.

'Now girls, could you sit over there, while we ask you a few questions.'

We do. David continues:

'You see CJ,' (he is talking to an older man, obviously boss around here), 'you see with the new TV regulations we have to use Equity members or real stewardesses for this type of job. As you saw from the other side,' (what does he mean?) 'these girls have the necessary glamour, and they are, I can assure you, trained stewardesses. Of course it may be imperative to put them on the books before we shoot, you know, just to keep the whole thing regular. But we here at Nutley, Bratwurst and Cutlet certainly believe that we have to personalize the whole travel syndrome. I mean if airlines are going to pull through this present recession, it is going to be a priority to establish an identity that will differentiate your airline from all the others. It is no longer enough to say that an airline can get you from A to B; that is now routine, we must have a Unique Selling Proposition. And ours is going to be the friendliness, with more than a hint of sex, of our cabin staff.'

Some of the young executives begin to twitch at the mention of the word sex.

CJ looks as though he may have fallen asleep, though perhaps he is keeping his eyes deliberately low so that he can observe my creeping bikini all the better. I can feel it going, but while David is talking so earnestly I daren't do anything about it.

'Our two-pronged assault on the market, our twin strategy you might say, is to sell a subconscious desire to treat the plane as a womb substitute with an almost up-market appeal as a real-man's airline.' It is no use – as he says two-pronged, my bikini top slips. It has been under considerable strain, and when it goes, I am left clutching at my front. I have quite large hands for a girl, but they are completely inadequate for the task.

CJ saves the day. 'The best two-pronged assault on the market I have seen all week.'

The executives trumpet and hoot with laughter; when CJ makes a joke, you better laugh, is the feeling I get. I slip on my shirt. My nipples are actually standing on end with embarrassment, a very strange sensation.

'OK, David,' says CJ, 'I understand the strategy. I agree with it, I have approved it long ago. Let's cut the crap. We are here to decide if these two girls are the right ones for our publicity and advertising campaign. I know about your literary efforts, Miss Sutton, and your previous employment with one of our rivals. We will not mention your names in the campaign, if we use you, just a first name. I am going to authorize an experimental budget of £10,000 to try out the first commercial with these girls. OK? If the whole idea is a bomb-out, well then it's back to the drawing board. I want to see the first films in a month. Understood? Shoot as soon as possible, research the films and let me have the findings one month from today.'

'That's a Sunday, sir,' says one young man.

A silence you could carve up and eat falls.

'Are you religious?' asks CJ.

'No sir,' says the young man.

'Well I suggest you start praying that you've seen the light by next month. Good morning girls.'

He sweeps out followed by the whole troupe, except for David who hugs us warmly.

'Well done, he likes you.'

He presses a button and a television screen appears from behind a panel. He presses another and says, 'run the tapes.'

There, in full colour, are Kate and me coming into the room, fooling about and changing. My God, and I'm not wearing any panties.

'The miracles of modern science,' he says nastily.

CHAPTER THREE

'You have to do something to grab them in this world. It's dog eat dog in the advertising business at the moment, hard times, batten down the hatches, pull in the belt all that sort of stuff,' says David as he has another helping of smoked salmon.

We are in what David describes as his local caf, in fact the Trattoria Preciosa, waiting for Jake to turn up from another assignment. It is by way of a celebration. And do we have something to celebrate! I mean it's not every day you get whisked from oblivion as what Kate calls a titillator to the giddy heights of international television commercial filming.

We don't spare ourselves the champagne, I am glad to say, and by the time Jake arrives, all safari shirted and knee-high suede boots, we are very merry.

'Hello Dave, hello girls,' he says, 'isn't this fantastic news?'

'Hello Jake,' we all chorus in unison.

'Well, I see you've made a good start, I think I'll have a few oysters to catch up, put a bit of lead in the pencil, then we'll go out somewhere nice, good idea?'

It sure is. Jake's idea of somewhere nice is a private club on a boat moored on the Thames. Modesty almost forbids me to tell what sort of a club it is. A small boat picks us up at the pier, and takes us out the twenty yards to where the larger one, a converted patrol boat is anchored.

'Gives you twenty minutes on the fuzz,' Jake explains.

'I once went out with a policeman,' says Kate, 'he had the biggest truncheon on the force.'

You can see how the ball of wit is tossed to and fro. Kate is by no means sober at this stage. In fact, although it only takes a minute to get out to the boat, she begins to go ominously pale.

'Nothing a sniff of this won't cure,' says Jake, producing a bottle from his pocket. We all apply one nostril and inhale deeply. It's like going into orbit.

'What the hell's that?' asks Dave, as he begins to laugh merrily, 'the last time I felt so good was when CJ zipped up his cock in the men's room at the Junior Carlton.'

I haven't a clue what he's talking about, but the effect of that little bottle is magical. The colour comes back to Kate's cheeks in a trice. Jake tells us it is smelling salts, or poppers, used by old gentlemen to aid sexual congress, is how he explains it. We are at the bottom of the steps of the boat, and a very peculiar young man, dressed in a camp sailor suit helps us on board.

'Hello Jake darling,' he lisps, 'who are the friends then, my goodness, here's a real man at last?' he says looking at Dave and completely ignoring us.

Before we go below, Jake takes us to one side.

'Look, this is a gay club, gay fellers, gay birds, but also a lot of straights, so be a little careful. It's fantastic fun, but very exclusive. You'll probably see all sorts of people you know, but here nobody tells tales.'

Down below is a discotheque, a cinema showing films continually, a bar and a beautiful dining room, just at water level.

At first, in the dark, we think it looks much like a normal discotheque, but then as we get used to the light, I realize that things aren't as they appear to be. When I see a well-known politician, the laws of libel prevent me saying who it is, dressed as a woman in a long dress with a boa, dancing with a young man in a sailor suit, very popular, my eyes practically pop out of my head. And there are at least three famous actors, all dancing with other fellers, including one in outrageous drag. Jake and I begin to dance, too. Curiously I find the whole atmosphere very sensual. I am just eyeing a very good-looking young man whose face is familiar, when I realize it's an actress, known the world over for her outspoken political attitudes, in a man's suit dancing with a very pretty blonde girl. She gives me a big, friendly, smile, and I bury my face against Jake's shoulder.

Kate is getting a bit out of control. She and Dave are dancing as though they were alone in their bedroom, but in this company it goes unnoticed. Jake leads me to another room, where there is a large television screen, showing camp blue movies.

They are all done with a sense of humour, but really I much prefer to be part of the action in life than looking on.

'Just one more drink before the cabaret,' says Jake.

'Anything you say; how about another sniff of that bottle?'

I have another deep sniff, and really feel unbelievably sensual for a few minutes. Jake gives me a deep probing kiss, and his hands slide over my breasts. I push my hips into him and slip my hand down the back of his trousers for a moment. His hand goes up under my skirt and begins to stroke my bare flesh. As everybody at Nutley, Bratwurst and Cutlet now knows, I don't always wear panties. We go into a little corridor and Jake tries the first door we find. He pushes it gently open. It is a little store room, full of paint, ropes and a drum of something. Jake pushes me in front of him, and shuts the door. He has my skirt around my waist and his trousers unzipped. We can only just get into the room, more of a locker really and I am beginning to wonder how we will get it together, when he turns me round and puts my hands on the drum. I feel as though I am about to play leap-frog, but suddenly he slips into me from behind. It hurts a little at first, but there is something very exciting bending over like this, and I find my hips pushing back to meet his. My heart is racing from the poppers and what is happening to me. It's all over in a flash, and I am in tears, tears of happiness if you can understand that. Jake is very tender; he wipes my face with his shirt tail, and we are back in the main room all within five minutes.

The cabaret is outrageous. It's done by the cast of a fashionable gay musical, singing and dancing to old rock numbers. All the men and all the women are dressed in black stockings, suspenders and waspie little corsets. It may sound bizarre, but the whole thing is hilariously funny and very, very blue. The girls in the show are bare breasted and the men, if you can call them men, are tall, thin and very beautiful. Obviously everyone here has seen the show, because they call for their favourite songs. Kate is sitting near me, her eyes popping out of her head. One of the girls in the show drags her up to the middle and they begin to strip her off. Just as I am laughing my head off at her plight I get seized upon.

'Now, Doris,' says the leader of the troupe, 'show us what you've got.'

I have no option, because they have got my top off already. But what happens if they come to my skirt? Jake realizes what I'm in for and he grabs an arm and starts to tug me off the platform. Kate has created a diversion by going into her go-go dancing routine with one of the other girls. It's no good, off comes my skirt – there is a huge roar of approval, or at least I hope it's approval, from the audience. Mercifully one of the cast gives me a long, dracula type of cloak. But by now all sorts of fun has broken out – the cast and most of the audience are dancing about like dervishes. I find myself dancing with a girl dressed only in a G-string and long black stockings. She tried hard to get inside my cloak with me, but fortunately Jake comes to my rescue.

'My goodness, what are you up to?'

'I'm not up to anything – I mean that in more ways than one, too.'

'These girl-guide parties get a bit rowdy, don't they?'

'Let's go and rescue Kate before she gets into a bisexual gangbang.'

Jake has no enthusiasm for another struggle, so we go off quietly to the shore and home. God, what an evening. I have a little conscience about leaving Kate with this lot, but Jake says Dave will take good care of her.

In the morning, I feel as though a herd of elephants had passed over me without pausing to ask the way. Kate is sitting at the end of my bed looking distraught.

'Hello my sweet, the PTA meeting go off OK?'

'Penny, I've got to talk to you.' Her magnificent front is heaving violently. How much of this will her denim shirt be able to stand?

'Kate, you come barging in here like a bull in a teacup.'

'China shop.'

'Storm in a china shop . . . well, anyway, you come barging in here, wake me up and then say you must talk to me. You are talking to me.'

'Penny, be serious. I am in trouble.'

'I told you not to go off the pill so soon.'

'Not that sort of trouble, you moron.'

'Well?'

Kate composes herself with an effort, turns away from me, stares disconsolately out of the window, at the tin bath on the next door roof, and says,

'I think I've gone gay.'

I begin to laugh uncontrollably. This is a bit like the Kray twins taking up crochet.

'What are you laughing at?'

'I'm not laughing, I'm dying of mirth.'

'Some friend you are. You're bloody useless to me.'

I try to control myself. Actually, if Kate has gone queer, there's no hope for the rest of us. I would not describe her as a nymphomaniac, not to her face anyway, but she certainly has had a fairly spectacular consumption of men in the years I have known her.

'Tell your Auntie Penny all about it.'

'Well, after you left, deserted is the word I am looking for, Dave and I went on to another party with some of the people on the boat and I found myself with this very good looking boy, in a fantastic Pierre Cardin suit, and one thing led to another. Well as he began to undress me, I thought, hello, there's something missing here. I won't tell you what, but he turned out to be a girl in drag. I had been with a girl for half an hour.'

'Kate, did this girl look like a feller?'

'Yes.'

'And did he, she, behave like a feller?'

'Yes.'

'And did you have any way of knowing it wasn't a feller?'

'Not until we got in the bedroom.'

'So there.'

'I had been snogging with this dyke for ages.'

'Well you can't blame yourself for that.'

'No, suppose not.'

'The day you turn queer, I'll become a nun and that's a promise.'

'I had to tell someone. I mean Dave gave me some very funny looks on the way home.'

'You haven't screwed up our job with him, have you?'

'No, I think he really is bi-sexual. If anything it will have turned him on.'

'Oh well, if that's the end of True Confessions for the day, could you make me some coffee. And while you're there ducks, give me plastic mac a wash. You'll find it behind the riding boots and whips.'

'Don't. Uggh. I feel so ashamed of myself. How in hell did we get in with that lot?'

'We always seem to find the lowest element, somehow, don't we?'

'Thank the Lord.'

Kate is incapable of being down for too long, and having poured out her heart, a pretty thin trickle, to me, she is as cheerful as ever in no time. Dave has told her that if we are a success in the first test film, they are proposing to use us as the symbol of the airline's service for about six months or a year. We will be under contract to him for photographic, film and personal appearances – and we will do a bit of flying just to prove we're real stewardesses. On promotional trips and things like that. Airlines have a habit of trying to get influential people on their side if they are opening up a new package holiday or a new route to somewhere exotic – they ask a group of people from television, the newspapers and public life and treat them like kings for a few days, so that they will spread the good news. We will be their official hostesses on one or two of these flights. It sounds fantastic.

I am more cautious than Kate, because we have learned that all that glitters is not gold, or even tinsel.

'Let's just make sure we do OK on the first bit, the test commercial before we get carried away.'

Jake calls round at that moment.

'Look, I'm off till tomorrow. Dave will make all the

preliminary arrangements. He wants to start shooting on Friday, because the whole schedule is very tight. So the next couple of days you will be in wardrobe and make-up and that sort of thing, and I'll be back on Thursday. We shoot in the flight simulator on Friday and then in Paris on Saturday, Sunday. See you.'

He gives us each a big friendly kiss. As he goes out of the door he pauses for a moment.

'By the way, don't be going out with any girls your mothers wouldn't like to have to dinner. Bye.'

It takes a moment for this remark to sink in, but it's too late, he's gone. All we can hurl after him is abuse.

After a sauna and a swim at a club in Mayfair, we go along to David's office for briefing and wardrobe.

David is very business-like, not a hint of the man who was dancing the can-can with a couple of young men dressed in black stockings and a garter belt. He does manage to give us a broad wink at one point. I reflect that he is very decadent but also very well-organized and practical, not a common combination.

It turns out that we will be filming, as Jake has said, Friday, Saturday and Sunday. First we have to do all sort of make-up and wardrobe tests. Pierre la Cloche, the famous make-up expert, does our faces and then we are filmed on video tape. We spend the whole afternoon changing our make-up. He is incredible – he can make you look like a wide-eyed schoolgirl one minute and a sultry, smouldering sex bomb the next. The Agency, naturally, goes for a look somewhere between the two. Then we try on uniforms, off duty clothes, beachwear, evening dresses and God knows what. You would think they were making Cleopatra not a sixty-second TV commericial, but I am most impressed by all the preparation.

The uniforms are sensational. Normally British airlines tend to dress their stewardesses like policewomen or traffic wardens, but these uniforms are something else. We are wearing the two prototypes for a whole new style. The room is cleared before they can be brought in, in a locked holdall. Only the wardrobe lady, Dave and us are left as they come out of their wrappings.

We try them on, the wardrobe lady makes adjustments with pins and they go back into their holder to be taken away somewhere and altered. It reminds me of Princess Anne's wedding.

Dave finally sends us on our way about nine o'clock. 'I imagine you both need a good rest. Tomorrow we start rehearsing at 6.00 am, so let's all get some sleep.'

'Make a change,' says Kate wisely.

CHAPTER FOUR

Never, never believe them if they tell you that the life of a film actor is easy. Photography sometimes seemed to me to be a bit complicated, but this is crazy. When we arrive at the studio at six am, yes six o'clock in the morning, it looks as though a hurricane has struck. There are people everywhere, generators, lights, carpenters, electricians and sundry hangers-on who don't seem to have anything to do just at present. Out of this chaos they appear to be trying to construct a large set. We are hurried off to make-up, where we sit, fully made-up, for two hours before Jake needs us.

'Just tests and rehearsals today. Lighting, camera equipment, that sort of thing,' says he.

'Good morning,' I say pointedly, as it's the first time I have seen Jake for two days.

'Oh hi.'

Kate and I exchange funny looks. Jake turns out to be very single-minded on the set, as they all call it. By the time breakfast comes along at nine o'clock, we still have not done anything. Everyone falls on the breakfast like peckish locusts, though there is a lot of grovelling and 'can I get you a cup of tea sir' for the important people, who don't include us. The technicians treat us like part of the scenery except for the cameraman, who is called Mike. He doesn't seem very interested in what's going on, but he's obviously got a sense of humour. He sits quietly watching two men struggle with one of those huge lights for half an hour, and when they've got them set up he says:

'Fred, let's move those lights to the other side of the studio.'

I can only assume nobody kills him with a blunt instrument because he's more important than they are. Anyway, he's very nice to us and quite good-looking, though a little short. Kate thinks he's a handy size, whatever that means.

After ages of pushing, pulling, moving lights, sets and cables, Mike is satisfied with the lighting and returns to the back of the studio to read *Tit Bits*. His job seems to be over. Occasionally he appears with something that looks like a small camera and peers through it at the set. He usually says F 8, which I take to be a secret code. Jake has been busying himself all this time with scripts, hurried conferences in dark corners of the studio and elaborate practice movements with the camera. His job seems to be to make it all as complicated as possible.

I ask him about this.

'Listen dearest, I get paid a lot of money, I have to make it look difficult, don't I, otherwise they would rumble me.'

This sounds reasonable to me. I've always tried to give value for money. Suddenly it's our turn to do something.

Jake shouts, 'Lights' and the studio is darkened. The backdrop lights up. Jake puts us in the middle of the set, and a howling gale begins. Our hair, which Pierre's assistant has spent loving care on is blown all over the place.

'What's that fucking wind machine doing?'

'Sorry, guv, pressed the wrong button.'

'Jesus, turn it off before somebody begins to sing Desert Song. Now get back to make-up and do your hair.'

Half an hour later we come back to find the continuity lady in hysterics. Her scripts and notes have blown all over the set. She is comparing this production unfavourably with The Forsyte Saga.

Just as we are getting back on our marks, bits of tape

where we have to stand, a huge lady in a tweed suit appears carrying two cat baskets.

'Sorry I'm late, dear,' she says to David, 'but one of the little buggers pissed on the conductor on the train.'

'What are you doing here, it's not Kitty-Delight today, that's next week Friday.'

'I have come all the way from Sevenoaks, I've groomed these cats, I've rehearsed the part where they jump on to the table sixteen times, and as far as I am concerned, it's Kitty-Delight today or Alfred, Snowy, Petal and Ding Dong will never eat that crappy rubbish again, which they hate anyway – my vet's bills for food poisoning are unbelievable, and you can take your bloody Kitty-Delight and feed it to the fucking hyenas in Whipsnade Zoo, maybe they would like it.'

She opens the cat baskets and four cats leap out. One, Alfred, an extremely large animal with a cynical expression, leaps on the remains of a bacon sandwich and devours it in record time. Its cunning eyes look around craftily for the next trick. The other three cats run like hares behind the scenery, one of them leaving a trail of vomit.

'Now look what you've done, you pip-squeak,' shouts the lady, giving David a clip round the earhole which sends him reeling. 'These are the most famous cats in Britain, and if they get damaged you're in trouble. Ding Dong, good pussy, come on Petal.'

Only Alfred is completely cool. He rips open a pack of Jaffa Cakes with a flick of his mighty paw and begins to tear them limb from limb. David shows unexpected signs of strength, however.

'Listen you old rat-bag,' he bellows, 'you better remember one thing, legally these cats belong to clients of Nutley, Bratwurst and Cutlet, and you are paid a fee to look after them. You may think you are Jimmy Chipperfield, but I can assure you, you are as useful on a film set as the Pope's prick, now get those cats out of here and be back here, as ordered next Friday, or I'll have the whole legal profession down in Sevenoaks with enough writs in their hands to paper your loo, if you've got one, which judging by the smell is unlikely.'

She wilts. 'Oh my God, I'm sorry Mr Sandstead. Since my husband died, I've found it a great strain, forgive me. The country is going to the dogs. I'm sorry.'

The film crew are very impressed by this argument. They stand about with their mouths open, hoping to catch flies, as my mother would say.

'What are you all standing about for. Find those bloody cats and let's get on.'

But it's lunchtime. After a tense, whispered conversation, which I can hardly catch, Jake shouts, 'OK, break for lunch.'

We go around the corner for lunch, Jake's assistant has very thoughtfully ordered it all. After all the excitement we drink too much, so that by the time we get to the studio again the atmosphere has changed considerably. The crew have been in the pub and those that are not asleep have a tendency to bump into things. Strangely enough, nobody seems to worry too much about the lighting any more. Mike is much more interested in helping Kate with her costume which involves lots of friendly hugs and tugs and nudges.

The afternoon passes in a flash. We stand in front of the camera, we sit, we walk about, we change our make-up, they change their lenses.

'It's a very good thing this rehearsal,' says Kate, 'I am getting quite used to the camera.'

'Perhaps there is some method in their madness.'

'I hope so. When CJ said ten thousand pounds for a test, I couldn't think how you could spend that much on a commercial.'

'The way we're going, they will spend that much on booze and food alone.'

The only time the crew shake off their lethargy is when we do some shots in our bikinis. Then they stand about like spectators at a punch-up. Full of suggestions, but obviously not really wanting to be part of the action.

'Let's get down to the simulator tomorrow good and early, so that the art department can get the whole place dressed in good time.'

It's another language to me, but the others seem to know what Jake is talking about.

'OK, it's a wrap.'

'I haven't got a wrap, not even an overcoat.'

The crew fall about laughing when they hear this.

'That means we can all go home now.'

I go into the dressing room and find Kate, wearing only a dressing gown and Mike going at each other as though they are trying to disappear down each other's throats.

'You lesbians are the worst.'

She looks up for a moment. 'I think that was just a phase in my life.'

'Look, get the midget out of my dressing room.'

Mike doesn't take this hard at all. He strolls off, giving me an affectionate pat on the bottom.

'Come round to the Engineer's for a drink when you're dressed.'

These film types just stagger through the day in order to get into the pub. It's one of those pubs where anything breakable has been stripped off the walls and anything which gets in the way of serious drinking has been discarded. Even the plastic flowers seem to be veterans of many a foreign war. The crew are lined up at the bar like junkies waiting for a fix. In their case the fix is usually taken orally in the shape of a large pint of wallop, followed by a whisky chaser. No wonder the film business is in such a bad way, at least that's what they all say continually.

The landlord tries to pretend he likes them, but the look of pain on his face as one of the electricians starts to remove his trousers says it all. Mike thinks this is his cue to get out and we go gratefully. I have to meet Jake later in the evening after his round of meetings and other business is over, but I begin to feel as spare as a pork chop in a synagogue the way Kate and Mike are looking at each other. Kate catches my glance and says:

'Well, I am so happy to find out that I am not gay after all, I want to make the most of it.'

There is something strange about her logic, but you have to admit it does make a mad type of sense.

'Well, I think I'll be off and go and change.'

'Don't go, no, no you're welcome to stay,' they say, practically pushing me out of the door of Mike's car.

'Don't worry about me,' I say, 'I'll get a taxi.' Mike's tail lights are already disappearing in the distance. That's the way it is with young love I suppose, the heart rules the head. A taxi with its light on ignores me. Bother young love. Randy animals.

My evening goes from bad to worse. Jake is two hours late and by the time he comes to get me I feel as though I am ready for breakfast, not a night on the town. But Jake is a man of surprises. He takes me straight home to his flat. He has ordered a meal from one of those dial-a-meal places, something very simple with lots of cold white wine.

'Well, how did you enjoy your day's filming?'

'To be honest, not a lot.'

'Don't worry, it gets better. Today was just a technical day. You'll enjoy Paris. Do you know it at all?'

As he talks he is caressing the inside of my thigh, which

makes normal conversation difficult.

'Yes. I used to fly there occasionally. I don't know it that well because I was in and out a bit too quick to do anything exciting.'

'As the actress said to the bishop.'

'Do you want to conduct a conversation or all-in wrestling?'

'Both.'

'Don't be greedy now. I'm a very single-minded girl. One thing at a time.'

His fingers have worked their way up inside my panties and are creating havoc.

'Yes, Paris is an exciting city. There is a whole lot to do there, like visiting museums and that.'

He is gradually removing my panties as he talks, non-stop. I am beginning to writhe, but I play the game.

'I particularly want you to take me to the Impressionist Art Museum,' I say, as I unzip his jeans.

'And a visit to the municipal sewers is a must for any tourist.' He is now getting to work on my blouse, unbuttoning it button by button. I have his belt undone.

'What about onion soup at four o'clock in the morning?'

'And what about a ride on the Seine.' I am now wearing only my bra, but he reaches round the back and begins to unhook that. I begin to slip off his briefs. As he talks, I slip down between his legs and take him in my mouth.

'Of course,' he says nonchalantly, 'you could also visit the flea market.'

I cannot reply, for obvious reasons.

'There again, a walk in the Bois de Boulogne on a fine day can be invigorating.' His hands reach down and cup my breasts.

Suddenly he says, 'I surrender.'

We roll on to the carpet and he begins to stroke my body

all over. I lie back with my legs spread out, my hands behind my back pretending to be indifferent. His lips move down from my nipples, over my stomach and between my thighs. I can contain myself no longer and my hips begin to work frantically. Still he stays down there. I come once, twice, three times, before he moves on top of me.

'Paris, here I come,' he says wittily. And he does.

CHAPTER FIVE

Kate insists on calling it the 'stimulator'. But it is really a stationary plane used for all sorts of training by airlines. Today it is painted in the new livery of British-American Airlines for our filming. The interior has been done up with lovely new upholstery, a chef from the head catering office is preparing the trays with a care I am afraid is never normally lavished on them, extras dressed as business men and holiday makers are swarming all over the place, electricians are moving lights about and Jake is presiding over the whole circus. All this for a commercial, and one that may never be shown.

'There's a lot riding on this,' says Dave.

'I can see,' says Kate, 'and most of them free-loaders at that.'

'I don't want to make you nervous, but you had better be good.'

'We'll try,' says Kate, thrusting out her chest dutifully.

'Morning all,' says Jake. 'This is the big one.'

For a moment I think he is talking about himself, but then I realize he's actually on about the filming. He takes us into the plane and we rehearse with a couple of extras, serving the dinners in the correct fashion. I am serving an old gentleman who is dressed like a priest, very sweet and saintly looking he is too. This goes on for half an hour.

'Right, into make-up and we'll start to roll as soon as you're ready,' says Jake.

It is very simple what we have to do. I bend over the old gentleman, hand him the tray, he gives me a warm smile, and I smile back. At least it sounds simple. Trouble is every time I lean forward, his dirty old eyes nearly pop out on stalks as he tries to look down my cleavage. Not that it is difficult. These uniforms have been designed to look sexy, and when I lean forward he gets a perfect view all the way to my navel. We both begin to get a bit hot and bothered under the lights as Jake makes us do it time and again. I am bending so far forward for the required angle that I practically dish my boobs up with the dinner. The priest looks more and more hot around the collar. Perhaps I should say dog-collar.

Mike and Jake confer, then they change the set-up.

'Look, when she gives you the tray, look at her face, smile one two, and look down at your tray. Not her tits.'

It is a funny way to talk to a Rev but then he isn't a real one. We try again.

'That's no bloody good. Are you an imbecile? Look at her face!'

'Take nine. Action.'

It's no good, the old goat is mesmerized by my boobs.

'Perhaps I should do this scene,' says Kate out of earshot of the priest.

'Don't be bloody silly. If you did it he would have a coronary. Let's give him five minutes to cool off.'

When I get in position next time to try again, I notice that his hat is on his lap, where it wasn't before. He does the whole thing perfectly, first time, until it is my turn to smile at him. He looks me firmly in the eyes, and lifts the hat, unseen by the camera. God almighty, I am amazed as much as shocked by the size of the thing. He should run the Vatican flag up it for church publicity. Fortunately, I manage to keep my cool long enough to finish the shot.

'Wonderful. Fantastic. You were both great, great. Right, let's get on to the bit where you bring the teddy for the kids, Kate. You can rest for a while Penny.'

The old man who is playing the priest goes off to the lavatory. I tell Kate what has happened and she bursts out laughing.

'You should have poured hot coffee on it.'

'Listen Kate, that old boy must be feeling faint from loss of blood to the head.'

'Why don't you go to the loo and see if he's all right.'

'I hope the teddy gooses you.'

'I would die if anybody touched me. That Mike is a demon lover. I feel like a bus ran over me.'

'You look like a bus ran over you.'

'Thanks.'

'That's OK. Just one thing. What happened to your mad, passionate affair with Dave?'

'I went over to his place after Mike left.'

'Did you . . .?'

'Ask no questions, get told no lies.'

She goes off to the other end of the plane where they are set up to film her giving the teddy to some children. I am getting a bit worried about Kate. I mean this is a hell of a pace to keep up. And how do Mike and Dave feel about sharing her? At least I seem to have Jake all to myself at last.

We are joined for lunch by CJ who is very cheery today.

'I have to confess,' he says, 'that this is a good day for us. We have just won a new contract to operate in the Pacific and South America which could make a lot of difference to our whole set-up. I believe that this is the continent of the future, and I hoped to be able to get a foothold there before any of our main rivals. Now we've got it.'

We all murmur enthusiastically. He is used to holding the floor, that's obvious, because no one else gets a chance to say a word for ten minutes. Even Jake seems to have been silenced. He rests his hand on my thigh and gives it a friendly squeeze.

'How's the filming going boys? How are these lovely young ladies doing?' He gives Kate a pat under the table. I only hope his hand doesn't meet Mike's, who is sitting over the other side of her. Perhaps even now their hands are locked in mortal combat over possession of her strategic points. I check myself. Really, I must get off the sauce at lunchtime. The mind begins to wander. With CJ the mind doesn't so much wander as go into hibernation. He talks and talks, and one of the account executives is the only person still looking interested by the end of the lunch. It is a positive relief to get back to the studio. Even the irrepressible Dave is repressed.

The afternoon involves us in little incidents with the passengers – a child crying so we get some comic books, baby needing changing, serving snacks and drinks. It's all going beautifully, until we hear some singing from one of the toilets.

'Get that noise stopped immediately,' shouts Jake. One of his faithful minions troops off to the back of the plane. There are some thumps and more shouts.

'What the hell is going on?'

'Sorry guv, but that old priest berk is locked up in the casi. He sounds a bit elephants to me.'

'Well get the bastard out of there, put him in a mini-cab and send him home to Lambeth Palace.'

'He comes from Cricklewood, not Lambeth, guv.'

'You'll be going with him if you don't get him out.' He goes back to the loo. We try to get on with the filming, but just as we are about to roll, there is a thunderous crash from the back of the plane and the whole of the toilet section falls to the floor, most of it on top of the assistant director, who has been trying to force the door open with a crowbar. The priest, wearing his shirt and dog-collar, and a pair of socks with suspenders, and that's the lot, comes rushing out brandishing a fire-fighting axe.

'I'll get the little oick,' he shouts, 'where is he, interrupting an ecclesiastical get-together, I'll excommunicate the infidel.'

The assistant director has enough sense to lie still under the wreckage of the economy class toilets. Perhaps it's not so much sense as the fact that he's virtually buried alive, that saves his life.

The mad axeman begins to make matchwood of the rear row of seats with the axe. He looks rather comical with his white spindly legs and his dog-collar. But if it goes on at this rate there won't be much of the plane left. He gets to work on one of the partitions. All the time he is coming closer to where we are working up the plane.

'Do something,' yells Dave.

'That's right,' Jake adds.

Mike grabs a fire extinguisher and lets the axeman have it with a blast of foam. For a moment this throws him completely.

'Manna from heaven. Manna, Hallelujah.'

He is really living his part. He falls on his knees and begins to scoop up the foam. Meanwhile the assistant director has extricated himself painfully from the wreckage behind and is creeping up on the priest. Before the priest can pick up his axe again, he rugby tackles him and holds him down.

They struggle for a while before the priest subsides, giggling to himself. Someone gets him a pair of trousers.

'Now what?'

'Get the police and take him to the funny farm. That's where he belongs,' says Dave.

'Nonsense. Get him a cab and take him home.'

44

After the treatment Mike has given him with the fire extinguisher, he looks as though he has been topped with whipped cream, and it's not a pretty sight. They struggle to get his legs into a pair of trousers, but he is still rolling about and laughing hysterically, occasionally letting out a whoop like an Indian on the warpath, and I mean a Red Indian not a bus conductor who discovers you haven't paid your fare. When they finally get him upright and wipe most of the foam off him, he has the trousers on back to front.

'Do you want me to walk backwards, Bishop?' he inquires of Jake who is beginning to show signs of impatience. At this moment the training officer from the airline comes up the steps and sticks his cheery face round the corner. His smile is exposed for a total fraud when he sees the wreckage.

'Holy Jesus, what have you done to our plane?'

'The Japanese launched a suicide attack, I am afraid,' says Jake.

'But I have to use this plane for training a new batch of stewards tomorrow.'

'Well I should train them somewhere else tomorrow. Now goodbye.'

We get on with the job in hand eventually, but it doesn't go too well. At least I don't think it's going too well, because we keep having to do things again and some of the extras begin to get a bit restless. They are all trying to be stars. As Kate says, it's a bit ridiculous when you realize the competition involved – I mean, we are the stars of this little lot.

By the time we wrap it up, my face feels as though it has been chiselled into a cheesy grin for the camera. The only bloke who seems happy to go on is Mike, perhaps because he has so little to do. But I discover later it's just that he hates going home.

It's all go. We have to pack for Paris, and get the late flight to the new airport. I explain to Kate that the sort of farewell she is giving to Mike isn't necessary, as she will see him on the plane, but it doesn't seem to have any effect. Naked lust is stalking the earth with these two around. And Jake always seems too busy during the day to pay me any attention. We go home and throw our things into two suitcases, grab a bite to eat and jump into a taxi. We meet over at Jake's place and drive off to the airport in his Rolls. It has quadrophonic sound and a cocktail cabinet, so well before we get to the airport we are a bit tiddly.

'The only way to fly,' says Dave, as he shakes up another batch of Martinis. Jake even manages to drink as he's driving, which I believe is illegal, but then as all the windows are of smoked glass, no one is going to see.

Suddenly the funny side of our day's antics begins to dawn on us as we drink more martinis. So much so that by the time Jake eases the Rolls into the car park, we are weak from laughter.

'Do you want me to walk backwards, Bishop?' asks Jake.

Mike is waiting to meet us with a mountain of gear he is checking through. The overweight bill is £400, but no one seems to care too much.

Finally we are airborne. I know one of the stewardesses from when Kate and I graced the airline in question, and she slips us all sorts of extras. The champagne and the martinis don't seem to get on too well, and I am soon in a deep sleep, my head on Jake's shoulder. As I doze off I hear Kate saying to Mike, 'Put it away, here, let me help.' I imagine she is talking about his light meter.

It is the first time I have been to the new airport in Paris – it's quite fantastic with stairways encased in tubes of plastic running up into the sky to transport the passengers around. Actually it's a bit bewildering finding your luggage. We've got so much of it that we employ half of the porters in the place to move it.

By the time we get to our hotel, a small but exclusive place with only nine rooms, each one really a small suite and often occupied by famous pop stars and the like, I am completely exhausted. Jake and I retire to our room, the Oscar Wilde Suite, and have a light supper, just oysters and wine, before slipping into bed. His energy is fantastic, and I am even more tired by the time we get to sleep, the two of us naked under a satin sheet.

CHAPTER SIX

The morning dawns all too soon. I have a slight headache, which is to be expected, I suppose, but it does not cheer me up to know that I deserve it. Jake, of course feels fine. So fine in fact that he has already had his breakfast and is doing push-ups on the floor, completely naked.

'Young man.'

'Yes, dear?'

'She is not there any more, you can stop now.'

'Ha, bloody ha. I fell out of me cradle right into the Mile End Road laughing at that one.'

'Give us a cup of coffee. Come on.'

He gets up off the floor and pours me a cup.

'What's the programme for today, chief?'

'It's all go today. The car comes for us in fifteen minutes and then we are off to the Eiffel tower, just so people who see the film know it's Paris, then various other location shops, then late night down to a discotheque in Montparnasse. Come on, get your arse in gear, we're in a hurry.'

He tips me out of bed. He looks rather appealing and boyish standing there naked, but there's no time for all that. Very sad.

As I get into my clothes, he comes up behind me, gives my breasts a squeeze and says, 'Be good today. I want these commercials to be great. OK?'

'I'll try.'

It's still only seven o'clock when we start filming at the Eiffel Tower. We are supposed to be stewardesses in Paris, enjoying our day off. The whole film is to be quick incidents, featuring Kate and me on duty and off, to give the airline a friendly, personal image.

Kate is holding up well under the strain. She has an unbelievable amount of staying power for one who throws herself so hard into the business of living, and loving for that matter. Ten times we stroll across the road, to the whistles of a man dressed as a gendarme before Jake is happy. The sun has to be in exactly the right spot behind the Eiffel Tower for him. Mike seems very little interested in what's going on, more in chatting up the French make-up girl.

'Voulez-vous coucher avec moi?' is the extent of his French, but he is trying it out with great enthusiasm. She just smiles.

We do a quick change in the make-up truck, now we are dressed for a trip down the Seine. Dave and Jake have hired a boat, one of those glass-covered jobs, and we cruise down the river to Notre Dame, causing chaos with the river traffic when we have to stop and reverse to do the shot again and again. The captain of the boat looks at me with a shrug, as if to say he always knew the English were crazy. I have pointed Notre Dame out to Kate seventeen times before Jake is happy. The captain has taken to shouting insults at passing boats before they can complain. He is beginning to lose his cool completely, and makes a rude sign at a police launch which comes up to investigate why we are going backwards in a narrow bit of the river. I don't know much French but there is a lot of talk about the English and lots of pointing at the head. The police go away, obviously convinced that any interference on their part will only lead them into tiresome complications with lunatics. Finally we break for lunch and go to one of those incredible French restaurants which just seem to be everywhere.

'Penny, I want to talk to you.' Kate seems to be a bit agitated again.

'Well go on.'

'Look, how can I get rid of Mike?'

'Get rid of him? I thought you loved him.'

'Not enough to want him to leave his wife and kids back in Neasden.'

'Is that what he's saying?'

'Yes. Last night. Quite put me off my stroke.'

'What were you stroking?'

'Now don't be crude. This is serious.'

'Nothing is so serious that it can't wait until I have finished my sole.'

'Quite the little gourmet, are we? You stuff yourself while I am in terrible emotional agony.'

'Darling, why don't you just have another drink while Aunty Penny thinks about your problem.'

I begin to laugh. Kate is sitting there looking all wide-eyed and distressed, but secretly I suspect she's enjoying the situation. I mean everyone likes to feel wanted, and if Mike is prepared to give up all that domestic bliss, nice little wifey, three kids, house in Neasden and a Siamese cat for Kate, that shows he really cares. Kate twists her napkin emotionally, but then she begins to laugh too.

'It makes a change, anyway, most of them think if they turn off Match of the Day for ten minutes while climbing aboard they are making a big sacrifice.'

'Don't worry, Kate, I'll think of something for you. I'll tell him your boobs are silicone or something.'

'Of course they're not.'

'I know that. Come to think of it, are you sure they're not?'

'Just because I am better endowed than you in this region,' she makes an appropriate gesture, 'there is no need to get nasty about it.'

'Them.'

'All right them.'

'Well, why don't you learn to live with it. You are so desirable that men will go mad and foam at the mouth if they can't possess you forever.'

'It's the forever that worries me.'

As we get on with the filming, now dressed for a visit to the Impressionist museum, I forget all about Kate's problem.

Jake has an ambitious plan this afternoon. It's called stealing a shot, he tells me, that is to say he doesn't get permission to film in the Place de la Concorde, but is going to snatch the shot on the run before the police can move us on. The idea is that Kate and I should try to cross the square, the biggest in the world says Dave, and he knows everything, when we see the camera car coming, in the direction of the museum. It sounds simple enough, but if you have ever tried to cross a windy street in a short shirt, that's one half of the problem. The other is that the Parisian uses the Place de la Concorde as a test track for speeding, braking and shouting at policemen and his fellow motorists. Just standing on the pavement staring across at the sea of hooting, struggling traffic makes me feel apprehensive. There are about twenty lanes of traffic, all of them trying to go in different directions. Even as we wait on the curbside for the camera car to make a circuit of the square, drivers begin to shout, wave, hoot and whistle at us. I am particularly vulnerable to the sports car driver standing on the high kerb in a very short skirt.

As the camera car comes into sight, five men standing on the top, a voice crackles on the assistant director's walkie talkie and he shoves us off into the traffic. Kate and I pretend to chat unconcernedly to each other, smile at motorists and try to look natural. As I thread my way through some cars, more than one hand finds its way up under my skirt for a quick feel.

'Not so much crossing the bloody Place de la Concorde as the Place de la Grope,' says Kate.

The traffic is piling up all round us. Suddenly there is a crash and the tinkling of glass. Two cars have bumped into each other. A driver gets out and begins to shout at the bloke behind him. A third car goes into the back of that one. The wind is tugging at my skirt, and Kate has abandoned trying to hold hers down altogether. All traffic comes to a halt. Whistles begin to blow as gendarmes arrive. Jake shouts from the top of the camera car, which is very close to the pile-up.

'Terrific. Give that cop a kiss Kate. That's it. Now piss off fast before you get arrested.' The policeman gets a big cheer from the motorists as Kate kisses him. We flee, leaving behind total chaos.

Over in the gardens where the Museum is we have a quick drink to help us recover from the excitement. After a lot of gesticulation and shrugging of the shoulders and fingers pointed at the head, the mad motor race starts up again in the square. It is so huge and so disorganized that it makes Hyde Park corner look like a village High Street on a Sunday afternoon. While we are waiting for the crew to get back to us, I explain to Kate my plan to get Mike off her back, and other parts.

'Look, it's very simple. When he comes to pick you up this evening, you are unavoidably detained elsewhere. I'll be in the room almost naked, you burst in as he's making a play, and you burst into tears. You are so shocked, you cannot see him again. Your best friend, too.'

'Did I know she was my best friend? Not until I found her sleeping with my boyfriend.'

'Sleep with him? Not me. He's a dwarf.'

'When did you get so fussy?'

'Do you want to get on with my plan or not? It's your bloody love-life I am trying to rescue from disaster. Mine's OK.'

'OK. You're right. But how do we know he'll make a pass?'

I give her a withering look. It's a bit like asking if a group of sailors on shore leave would pass up Raquel Welsh in favour of a nice read in the local library. That's what I try to imply in a look.

Kate is not terribly impressed. 'Well don't go too far.'

'Why not,' I ask, 'I thought you didn't like him any more?'

'That's not the point, Penny, and you know it.'

I do understand actually. A married man once said to me. 'Look, I can't stand my wife, but for God's sake don't you run her down or I'll get angry.' Likewise nobody likes you pinching their ex-boyfriends. Strange thing that, isn't it?

That evening we are off for four hours before we go to a discotheque on the Left Bank, at about twelve.

'Get some kip,' advises Jake, 'we are likely to be very late tomorrow morning and I don't want you two looking completely shagged out by the time we start to film.'

'OK darling, see you later.'

'Now Kate, you get old Mike to come up here in half an hour or so. I'll tell him you had to go to wardrobe, then you give us about ten minutes and come in. I guarantee as a friend there will be some action.'

'That's what worries me.'

Kate rings Mike and asks him to come up to her room before they go out for a drink. I strip off and put on my sexiest panties, tiny black satin, and a black, three-quarter bra which pushes my boobs up practically to my chin. I scent myself all over with Eau Sauvage, and lie on the bed with the light down low.

After a few minutes, the door pushes open. I pretend to be asleep, lying on my back with my legs apart. Actually, lying there brazenly is beginning to turn me on. Mike is obviously a bit taken aback. He turns to go. I turn sleepily and say: 'Mike. Is that you?'

'Yes. Where's Kate?'

'Come in, she said she was sorry but she would be about an hour.'

'OK, I'll come back, sorry to disturb you.'

'That's OK. Stay, and you can pour me a drink, there's some champagne in the bidet keeping cool.' I cross my legs suggestively. When he comes back with the champagne, I have the sheet pulled up to my waist. We both drink out of the bottle and he sits on the bed. I reach across him for a cigarette, and it is too much for him to bear. He kisses me.

My hand is on his thigh, and I squeeze it gently.

'Naughty, what would Kate say?' I lie back on the bed, the sheet now around my knees. Mike swings his legs up on to the bed, and kisses me again. I turn my head away in mock horror, but one of my legs is between his thighs. He has his jacket and trousers off in a flash. Help! This is all going a bit too quickly. Got to hold him off for five minutes, or the way this lad is straining at the leash it may be too late by the time Kate comes back.

The next few minutes are like visiting time at the snake-pit. Mike, now wearing only his scants and his socks, is swarming all over me. I let him get my bra undone, though I hold it to my chest. He is obviously not used to this sort of coy treatment: come to think of it, nor am I. Last time I carried on like this was in the back of an Anglia just after I had done my 'O' Levels. I am beginning to get very hot and steamy, particularly when his digits find their way inside my black satin panties. It all comes back to me over the years, how difficult it is to protect your top and your

54

bottom from a determined attack. I feel thirteen again. I also feel the hot, insistent probing of Mike Feywick whose scants are no longer containing him at all. Every instinct in my body tells me to slip off my panties and draw him to me, but I know I mustn't.

'Down boy. What sort of girl do you think I am?'

'I think you're terrific. Now come back here.'

'Just getting some champagne, hold on to yourself.'

I try to stall him for a few more minutes as we drink champagne. Where the hell is Kate? This is unfair on both of us. Not to mention his wife and kiddies in Neasden, which we won't and don't.

Mike is getting angry. I can't blame him really. I ring the dinner bell, he gobbles the hors d'oeuvres and then waits impatiently for the main course and I say no deal. I decide to give Kate a few more minutes grace, then I can no longer answer for my actions. Mike's actions are being more and more direct. I have given up altogether trying to protect my top from his caressing fingers. His caressing lips follow in short order.

'What's the matter? You know you want to.' This boy has got a keen, penetrating mind. His keen penetrating fingers are at it again too.

Sorry about this, Kate, I think to myself, as I raise my hips to allow him to slip off my panties, but you brought it upon yourself. And me.

By the time a flustered Kate appears on the scene, her taxi has struck an onion seller, or something, I am lying in bed practically unconscious and the demon lover Mike has long since gone back to his own quarters. In fact there is such a glow of contentment about me that I can barely compose my face into a serious look for Kate's benefit.

'Oh my goodness, Penny, I am sorry. I just popped out to speak to Dave and the bloody taxi hit something.'

'That's all right, Kate old friend.'

'Did it go all right?'

'Fine, except you forget that you were supposed to appear.'

'Sorry – still we can do it tomorrow.'

'Kate, I don't know how to tell you this, but tomorrow will be too late.'

'What do you mean?'

'I mean Mike is leaving his wife and kiddies in Neasden for me.'

'For you?' She sounds absolutely amazed.

'Well, he was prepared to leave them for you, wasn't he?'

'That's different.'

'Shut up and get the champagne. We'll both tell him how irresponsible he's been and how we don't want to talk to him again. Your problems are over.'

Trouble is, I would love to talk to him again.

CHAPTER SEVEN

We film in a discotheque called Estelle. The joke is, so Jake tells me, that Estelle used to be a well-known boxer in France before she had a sudden change of heart. It's now the chicest thing in Paris and for our night's filming we have taken it over, although those of the regulars who don't mind a film crew about are there drinking free. Dave and Jake have also hired about thirty extras, models mostly, to dance and lounge about for the camera. The trouble they go to for a shot that will last about two seconds in the ad is incredible. We each have the most fantastic new dresses from a boutique in Paris, specially fitted for us.

'Penny, look over there.'

'Standing by the bar?'

'No, coming in the door? Isn't he an actor?'

'He was in that film where the boy slept with his mother, wasn't he?'

Kate is right, it is an actor but I don't go to French movies all that much so I can't remember his name. All French actors are called Jean-Paul or Jean-Claude, so Kate tells me. When it comes to do with anything male, Kate is usually right. Mike is pretending he hasn't seen us and is busy with the lights. You would think he was light-ing the inside of the Albert Hall, there are so many cables and lights about. Kate and I go up to him.

'Hello Mike.'

'Hello girls, I am very busy now, do you think we could talk later.'

'Oh this won't take a minute, Mike,' says Kate, 'it is about Neasden. Penny and I have decided that you shouldn't give up all for us, we're unworthy of your deep passion and single-minded devotion. And anyway, you couldn't marry both of us – bigamy is still a crime, although I believe the Liberals are going to legalize it when they come in.'

'Yes, well, out of the way now won't you – yes put that brute arc there, oui la, comme ca, oui you idiot.' Mike tries to get on with the job in his normal fashion; obviously we have scored a deep, wounding hit. We leave him berating the French technicians in a mixture of English and French; for all the understanding he's getting it might as well be pidgin Urdu.

Purely in order to rub some salt in his wounds, we go and chat up the French actor, who is called Jean-Claude as Kate has predicted, and like all actors is delighted to be noticed even though he is ostentatiously wearing a pair of outsize dark glasses. It's rather like one of those Minis with smoked glass windows – when you spot one you peer inside to see who it is. Behind his smoked glass windows, Jean-Claude is a bundle of Gallic charm and cool. He asks us politely what is going on and seems relieved to find out it's only a commercial. We introduce him to Jake who is suitably impressed. And then the work starts. Our training as go-go dancers stands us in very good stead for the dancing sequences. The same record goes on time and again and we dance away until the wee hours, trying all the while to look fresh and cheery. Long before we have finished, Jean-Claude leaves, but my heart gives a little skip when he asks for my hotel room number as he gets his coat.

Jake has the look of a fanatic about him this evening (or morning really) and he isn't content until we have done everything hundreds of times. As I stand there waiting to be told to dance for the umpteenth time, I wonder about him. I am very fond of him and it is terribly easy to talk to him but I get the feeling that this is only the surface. I don't really know anything about him. There seems to be a whole other side to his life which no one has informed me of. When we are in bed making love he seems to be elsewhere although he is a skilled and considerate lover. Maybe we have just seen too much of each other the last few days.

'What's the matter, Penny?' asks Kate.

'I don't know. Be serious for a minute. What do you think of Jake?'

'That's a funny question. It's you who have been seeing him so much. He seems OK to me, very good-looking, very rich, very easy to get on with, all that sort of thing. Of course I only had that one little fling with him when we first met, but he seems pretty terrific in the sack too. Actually, as I say all this he sounds like Mr Perfect. So what's bugging you?'

'There is something about him that I can't quite get hold of, no I'm serious not that, it's just that he seems so distant – he'll never talk about anything serious.'

'You're falling in love again.'

'I don't think so. Nothing that a touch of the Jean-Claudes won't cure.'

'He asked me for my number.'

'And mine.'

'Well, let's wait and see if he calls. Most unreliable these actor chappies.'

The sun is rising over Paris by the time we finish. What a beautiful city it is. We drive to the old market for breakfast. Jake is so relaxed and happy now that we are finished. He hugs Kate and me and pays us compliments by the score. We breakfast on onion soup, ham and eggs, lots of hot coffee and cognac.

'You girls were terrific. I can't wait to see the rushes. Don't you think so, Dave?'

'They were great.'

Dave is a funny one too. He seems to have gone off us a bit since that night on the boat in London. Perhaps after what Kate did it's understandable but I think it's more that he's bored with us. As Jake tells me later, he really doesn't have so much to do when the filming actually starts – he's more the organizer and fixer before the event, but I must say he has become a bit moody of late.

'You girls go back to the hotel and get some sleep – we'll get the plane back to London tonight. I'll be seeing you. Dave and I have some meetings. Mike you take care of them. Cheers.' And they are off – meetings, conferences, they're always off on little missions together.

Kate and I get our make-up off, take a long hot soak and jump into the same big bed in her suite. We sleep the sleep of the dead until midday.

Kate reaches across me for the phone. 'Yes. Oh yes. We would love to. I am sure she would too. No, no I'll tell her. When? This evening. OK, great. That's terrific, we'll see you then. Bye. No, she's still asleep, don't worry I will tell her. About six. Goodbye.' She puts the phone down. 'Penny, wake up.' She is so excited she is bursting out of her nightie.

'I am awake, what was all that about?'

'Jean-Claude has asked us down to St Tropez to his villa. I have accepted.'

'What about Jake and Dave?'

'Well they have got to get back to London and do their thing. We have nothing to do for a while.'

I warm to the idea of some sunshine and relaxation for a few days, and Jean-Claude and his friends should be exciting. Perhaps we will meet Brigitte Bardot.

'Perhaps we will meet Brigitte Bardot,' says Kate.

'It's all topless down there on the beaches.'

'We'll be OK,' says Kate smugly, and I know what she

means. In fact I wonder if we aren't just a little too big for the topless bit. It seems to me that in all the pictures of St Tropez I have seen all the girls are very slim with tiny breasts. Well they are in for a bit of competition now.

It is shameful the way we abandon Dave and Jake, not to mention Mike and promise to see them in London in a few days. Kate almost says we've got bigger fish to fry when they ask us why we're staying, but I tactfully jump in and say we just fancied a few days in the sun. Jake doesn't seem to mind – that curious blank look comes over him: even though he is smiling and kissing us goodbye I know his mind is somewhere else altogether. I really can't figure him out at all, but I am sure that somewhere deep down something is worrying him. Still, it's a little bruising for the ego that he doesn't insist I come back. Only Mike seems sad to see us go, but then he is off somewhere else tomorrow filming.

Jean-Claude arrives in a Maserati to take us to the airport. He is so good-looking he almost glows. Of course in Paris everyone knows him but he just waves them aside courteously, even the speed-cop who stops us on our way out to Orly airport.

'I 'ave only a few days in my villa, but you can stay as long as you wish. I am sure we get on very well, yes.'

'Yes,' we chorus as one girl.

It suddenly occurs to me that he thinks we are easy game for a threesome for a few days. I try to put the thought out of my mind on the flight south, but it is a bit worrying. I corner Kate near the loo on the plane and ask her if she thinks that is what he has in mind.

'Let's wait and see and play it by ear.'

Jean-Claude is tall and slim with wavy darkish hair brushed back in the 1930s style. He is obviously quite used to being adored by everyone, and Kate and I soon fall under his spell. He just assumes that you think he's marvellous and proceeds from there. Naturally, we are flattered to be with him even though I have a terrible suspicion that he is using us. On the other hand he must be able to get any girl he likes in St Tropez and anywhere else, so I try to tell myself that he must like us as well. In fact he is so charming and kind to us that my suspicious mind wonders all the time what his angle is. Still, if it's just sex, then Kate and I can handle it, no pun intended.

His villa in St Tropez is quite the most beautiful house I have ever seen – all white-washed walls, fur rugs and little courtyards and patios. Jean-Claude has a housekeeper and a butler down there permanently, and they greet him like old friends rather than servants. He embraces the old Lady, who is called Lydie, and she leads us like children to the dining room where a huge log fire is burning brightly. One side of the room is all glass looking out over the old port and to the lights on the bay.

'She says to tell you that you are two very lovely girls and she welcomes you in Provence.'

'Thank you.'

Jean-Claude tells us that he was brought up in Marseilles, an orphan, and Lydie and Francois look after him now that he is famous and rich.

'Do you enjoy the fame?' asks Kate brightly.

'Frankly, yes, I do. Perhaps when you come up from the gutter, like I 'ave you are more grateful for success.'

'I can see that,' I say, foolishly. But I can see that someone who had no family as a child should feel insecure. My heart warms to him even more than it is already, what with the rosé and the marvellous fish soup, really a whole meal in itself.

'Whenever I get the opportunity I come down 'ere to Provence and this is where I feel most at home.'

After the bouillabaise he grills some steaks himself on a

fire of vine twigs, and talks and talks. He is actually of Corsican descent, like Napoleon, but from the moment he could read he wanted to be an actor, a great actor.

'Now I am not so much a great actor as maybe I wished, but I am more famous and rich. Like your Richard Burton, in a way. Of course I am much younger than Richard Burton.' Of course.

Despite the fact that he likes to talk about himself, he is also very interested in us. It seems that there is a lot of kudos in having a few English girls around in France. He says this in the nicest possible way so that you can't object. I mean perhaps mama would not like it, but how often do you find yourself staying with a famous film star whom you hardly know. If he's asked us to be little mascots for a few days, that's OK by me. It's obviously OK by Kate, too, who is gazing at him as though she's expecting him to reveal details of the second coming at any moment.

'You English girls have, how shall I say this, you 'ave such a gentle way with you. French girls are very 'ard, very conscious of everything.'

Is this a compliment? Yes. Another glass of this wine and he could read me the telephone book and I would be flattered.

To our amazement, possibly even disappointment, Jean-Claude eventually says he is tired and needs an early night. It's not very early, but we have also had a few hard days in Paris, so off to bed we all go. Kate and I have a little guesthouse across a courtyard. Lydie has laid out some fresh fruit, some flowers and some mineral water by the bed.

'Penny?'

'Yes?'

'What's wrong with us?'

'I was wondering the same thing.'

Human nature is perverse. Here we are worried because he has not made a pass at either of us.

'Do you think he just doesn't like women or has had too many or what?'

'Kate, now don't get yourself in a tizzy. He is probably genuinely tired out. Anyway, the way you've been going at it the last few weeks a night's rest can't do you any harm my girl.'

'Thank you Sister Penelope. Over and out.'

I turn the light out and lie in bed thinking about the last few days. There is something very definitely odd about Jake and Dave and the whole set-up. I can't put my finger on it, but I feel faintly uneasy about it. I was getting on so well with Jake and then came a sort of freeze. They both seemed so distracted the last few days, so distant. Perhaps it's the pressure of work. But as I doze off, I know I am missing Jake already.

CHAPTER EIGHT

St Trop, they call it. We don't see much of it the first day. What we do see leads me to believe that the French are very, very rich. Fortunately I don't have to pay for anything, but everyone we meet seems to be rolling. By lunch time, Jean-Claude's drive is littered with expensive cars. In fact one very good-looking young man in cut-off Levis (actually they look as though they were made to look as though they were cut-off, if you see what I mean) who arrives in a mere Alfa Romeo abandons his car hastily amongst the Lamborghinis and tries to make an unnoticed entrance.

The drive is littered with expensive cars, and the pool-side is littered with expensive bodies. The girls are fantastically beautiful, little round bottoms and pert, French breasts. I feel a bit like a whale as I come out self-consciously in my monokini. Still, even in this world-weary group Kate and I cause a bit of a stir. I am so grateful to Maurice Bussman for those months of gyration I could kiss the little bleeder if he were here, which he isn't. We must make a pretty impressive pair, or pair of pairs, as we walk down the poolside together.

Jean-Claude introduces us around with, I believe I notice, a proud air, like a man who has just acquired a new car or a painting. I dare say amongst the St Trop jet-set he has gone up two ladders. Next time it will have to be three English girls to stay in the game. Hell, I don't care, they are all interesting and rich and attractive. What more could a girl ask for?

Lunch is served on board Jean-Claude's boat, a huge

ocean-going cruiser. It even has a waterski boat on deck. When we are well out into the bay, in the lee of a little island, they lower this boat and we all have a go at water-skiing. Jean-Claude advises the girls to wear a wet-suit on their tops, for obvious reasons. Kate practically skis under-water all the way to Cannes before she lets go of the tow-rope. Patrick, the poor one with the Alfa, comes with me. He is such a good skiier that he can stand on his skis and hold me up at the same time. It's fantastically exciting once you get going. Without Patrick's strong arm around me I doubt if I would be able to stand up at all – even with his strong arm around me I am quite exhausted long before we stop. His strong brown thighs, one of which finds its way against mine as we ski, mesmerise me.

'Enough Patrick, ça va, oui stop,' I cry in fluent French.

'Let it go.'

'I am not touching it, what are you talking about?' Witty old me.

'The line – let it go.'

'Oh the rope.'

We sink into the warm blue sea as the boat sweeps round to pick me up. Patrick has a ski on his own – he's a terrible show-off, but then as he's not as rich and famous as the others, perhaps he has to make up for it by being the best skiier.

'You 'ave enjoy it?'

'Thank you Jean-Claude, I have enjoy it enormously.'

'Bon. Come I wish you to meet somebody.'

'Love to.'

'Somebody' is a very beautiful woman, about forty I would say, who has lived a lot but still retained her looks. She is a very famous writer in France, who made a name for herself when only nineteen. It is she who has looked after the career of Jean-Claude, introducing him to all the right people, educating him so he tells me, teaching him how to dress and even wangling him into films for which she has written the script. Of course now he does not need the help any more, but they are such great friends. I can't help wondering if they were ever lovers, or are lovers.

'I wanted you to meet Jacqueline. She is my only real friend.'

'Silly boy.'

'Without her I would be a small gangster in Marseilles.'

'Dead, more likely.' She smiles at him affectionately.

'Allez, Janot, I wish to talk with Penelope.'

Off he goes like a little boy. She turns her attention to me, and somehow I feel uncomfortable in my monokini, even though all the girls on the boat are topless. She touches my arm as she talks. She has such a fierce interest in everything, particularly England.

'Is it true you eat marmalade with roast beef?'

'Not me.'

'I have never been to England, you know, 'ow do you say, because I am afraid I poison my liver on the food?'

'Well, the food's not like here in France, but it is not that bad.'

' 'Ow is she called, your friend?'

'Kate. Katherine.'

'Very beautiful girl, like you.'

'Thank you.'

Suddenly I have a horrid thought, if she is Lesbian and has such an influence over Jean-Claude, perhaps that is why he has brought us down here, to please her. He treats us with great respect and kindness but really doesn't seem interested in us in THAT WAY. Pity. As she grabs me by the arm again to make a point, I wonder how we get ourselves into this sort of situation.

'How do we get ourselves into this sort of situation,

Kate?' I ask her later when we are changing for dinner. 'An asexual actor and his mother figure, a raving dyke, and here we are stuck with them in the South of France.'

'Don't worry honey we'll find a way.' Kate is not finding a way into her T-shirt, which simply can't contain both her boobs at once. 'Help me get this thing over my head,' she begs.

'Kate, I think it would be better if you wore something, how shall I put it, more your size. It might be a red rag to a bull if you go out in that.'

'You can talk. That blouse looks as though it used to belong to Twiggy's little sister.'

'Be serious. If we are to survive this we have got to stick together, OK? Don't let's be separated – I don't want to end up in Marseilles, on my way to a harem in Majorca.'

'Morocco, darling.'

'That too.'

Actually we are a little intrigued to find out what the St Trop jet-set do of an evening, even if we do have to run the risk of Jacqueline springing some little surprise on us.

Mostly, it seems, the St Trop jet-set do what other people do on a night out. They drink a lot, eat a lot and try to get into each other's knickers. The trouble is they don't seem to care too much about the division of the sexes into male and female, something that Kate and I have always regarded as one of the few useful categories in life. But I am getting ahead of the story.

When Kate and I manage to overcome the problem of getting our well-fed frames into our respective clothes, we emerge on to the terrace by the pool to find a glittering party in progress. A huge barbecue is going on with chefs in white jackets and, for some reason, white scarves, cooking their tiny heads off. All that skiing has made me quite peckish so I fall on some fresh grilled sardines as though there were no tomorrow.

Jacqueline catches my eye, and then my arm, and drags me off to a tiny alcove at the other end of the pool.

'You are a beautiful girl, much too good for these 'orrible men.' She is drunk. I escape with just a little kiss in search of some 'orrible men to look after me.

Patrick, his Levis now changed for a beautiful cotton suit appears.

'For God's sake, help me.'

'Jacqueline?'

'Yes.'

'Don't give a tinker's curse for 'er.'

'Where did you learn your English?'

'Tinker's curse is not idiomatique, no?'

'Forget it. Help me get away from her.'

'Don't worry about her. She will pass out in a few hours. Just try to be quite nice to 'er before that time, or else she can make trouble with Jean-Claude. She is his mentor.'

I haven't really got much clue what he is talking about, but the boy has such a lovely delivery, I don't care. I grab him by the arm and lead him off to the buffet. I need to get a few drinks inside me before I can risk running into Jacqueline again.

'Penny, for Christ sakes, Penny.' Kate is looking hot and bothered.

'I know, you got groped by Jacqueline.'

'How do you know?'

'The same thing just happened to me.'

'She told me I was the most beautiful girl here.'

'Me too.'

'Well we are obviously both the most beautiful girl here. Here's to us.'

Patrick joins in our toast. ''Ow do you say. Cheers, no?'

'That's the idea. Or you can say bung-ho, down the hatch.'

'Bungo down 'atch.'

He is so good-looking I wish he would give up his English lessons and pay me some attention. Or go away and enrol in Berlitz.

Jean-Claude comes over, 'Try and be kind to Jacqueline. She is quite 'armless, and anyway she will soon be asleep. I am sorry if she embarrasses you but everyone 'ere is used to her.'

'OK, we'll try.'

Actually Jacqueline soon pales into insignificance compared with some of the characters we meet. They obviously believe because they are rich, successful and French that we are laid on by the management for their amusement, both male and female. It's like a party in the reptile house at Regents Park Zoo and the women are worse if anything than the men. Still, for the first hour or two it is relatively under control, but by the time the food is finished and the moon is up above the Mediterranean, people are swimming naked, dancing topless, or sitting round the fire listening to a well-known French singer sing his sad little songs.

I see Kate wearing only a tablecloth tied round her middle, Polynesian style, going off with a group of about five men and girls to the house.

'What's going on?'

'My policy is, if you can't beat 'em you might as well join them.'

She disappears into the house. I am beginning to feel the same way, particularly as Patrick, now back to his shorts again, is rubbing his hairy chest against my near naked front as we dance. I am getting quite hot and bothered when Jean-Claude comes over and takes me off for a dance himself. Patrick just steps aside dutifully. Jean-Claude holds me close and we dance overlooking the bay almost as though we were welded together. Here I am dancing with a man whom half the women in the world would give their right arm to be with. So when he leads me gently towards his bedroom, how can I possibly object? I can't. In it is a huge circular bed, covered with a beautiful Indian rug of soft wool. We lie on it and he gives me a drink. He turns on the television beside the bed, bloody funny time to be watching Z-cars I think, but it is a closed-circuit. He can see what is happening in every room in the house. And he does. In full colour. I feel a little sorry for Kate – she seems to be the centre of attention in her room, completely naked with two men and a girl on the same big bed. As we watch, the action gets ever more agitated. One of the men is on top of Kate while another is massaging her breasts vigorously.

Jean-Claude leaves the telly on and begins to undress me. It is quite a simple operation as I am only wearing a blouse, already open to the waist and my bikini bottom. We turn to another channel on the television, and there is Jacqueline, with two young girls, no more than seventeen and slightly Arab looking, completely naked. Jean-Claude laughs and turns off the television.

As a lover he is useless. He is so self-obsessed that he just wants to lie on his back and watch me work. Which I do with a will because I am feeling incredibly turned-on. When I try to kiss him he pushes my head down towards his middle. Well, he is the host after all, so I take him in my mouth. It can't go on long like this and it doesn't. He gives me an affectionate pat on the head and leaves the room. I am speechless. And also very, very randy. If they can behave like this, so can I. I wrap myself in a bathrobe and go outside and look for Patrick.

'Patrick.'

' 'Ello Penelope.'

'Do you wish to teach me some French?'

'Bung ho, down the 'atch.'

'Very good, Patrick, now come over here.'

'Do you wish to 'ave your lesson with your bathrobe on or off?'

'Off I think, today.'

'Shall I start 'ere.'

'Yes, that will do for a start.'

' 'Ow about here.'

'Very good. You are parlez-vousing a treat Patrick.'

'And here.'

'Oh yes, that is very good French.'

'My goodness, but you are a naughty girl.'

'Now teacher, I want you to combine your French with my English.'

'Like this.'

'Oui. And more oui.'

Patrick's lean, hard body is above me. There is no need for me to help him slip into me I am so wet with excitement. Those brown hips churn and mine rise to meet him each time, until we achieve a very effective rhythm. All that waterskiing has done him a power of good. By the time he lies quiet next to me, I have come three times. We lie back happily, enjoying a smoke, when a voice comes out of the TV screen. It is Jean-Claude, the idol of France.

'Very good. Very athletic. Bonne chance.'

Patrick gives the TV screen a French version of a Harvey Smith. Funny thing is I don't give a damn who is watching. Except my mother, and as far as I know she is tucked up in bed at this time of night with a cup of Horlicks and my old dad snoring away in his flannel pyjamas back in Blighty. Talking of Blighty, I wonder if Jake and his merry men are all OK. It is curious how you can be in bed with someone and find yourself thinking about another feller altogether. But I don't get a chance to let my idle thoughts wander for long because there is Patrick again, obviously rarin' to go. He caresses my breasts, takes a nipple in his mouth and away we go.

CHAPTER NINE

London seems a bit drab at first after all that excitement in France. We are back to do some flying, promotional trips for the airline. It's all got to be kosher, Dave has explained. Which means that if we are to be stewardesses in the commercials, we have to be real stewardesses on the airline, not just models. So CJ has arranged for us to go on a promotional trip, with an invited party in the first class, to Hawaii and back. Today we are to meet the rest of the crew and get a briefing.

London may seem a bit drab, but both Kate and I notice that Dave and Jake are not themselves at all. And it's nothing to do with jealousy either. They don't seem able to concentrate on anything for long, and they certainly don't have time to take us out and hear all about our experiences in St Tropez, which we are dying to tell them in a casual fashion.

'Jake, how are you?'

'I'm fine, Penny, and you?'

'OK. Would you like me to come round?'

'No, look I'm a bit busy at the moment. You know how it goes.'

'We had a lovely time in France.'

'Great. Now, look I'll give you a bell in a few days. Did Dave tell you we got some more films to do. Yeah? Good. OK, bye now.'

I know the brush-off when I see it. I almost wish I had stayed in St Trop with Patrick. He was all for it, with his lovely little cottage in the hills; I might have made a very good little French wifey, if only I could have got used to all that garlic. Patrick is an artist. In France that seems to cover a multitude of sins, but far from starving in a garret, his friendship with the stars has meant that he makes a lot of money. From time to time he paints portraits at huge prices, and for the rest he does Provençal landscapes. I am no art connoisseur, but he seems pretty good to me. Kate and I lingered on for five days down there until finally Dave got hold of us and told us to get back fast if we wanted our contracts to be maintained.

So here we are, about to go out to Gatwick to meet the rest of the crew.

'This is Lucy, Mandy and Kerry.' What bloody funny names, I think.

They smile at us as though they wish we were in a concrete box twenty miles off Land's End. Still, it is understandable. They do all the work and we grab all the publicity and the super trips to Hawaii. But it's not our fault so I wish they would stop arching their tatty eyebrows like that.

'You and Penny will look after the passengers in the first class, with their help. There are going to be lots of photographers and journalists from the travel papers – every one a soak and a bum – but I am sure you can handle them.' This is CJ's assistant talking, a man so neatly pressed I couldn't be surprised if he puts his pubic hair in curlers at night. Lucy, Mandy and Kerry look as though they have a bad smell under their noses as we come out in our brand new uniforms.

'We don't normally tie our scarves like that, dear,' says Kerry to Kate.

'Well tough titty,' says Kate pleasantly.

'For Chrissake, Kate, let's not get their fur rubbed the

wrong way at this point in the proceedings. We have to spend five days with these girls. It's only human that they should be a little jealous at first, until they realise what warm, sensitive human beings we are underneath it all.'

'I particularly don't like that little one over there, Mandy,' says Kate, 'she had better watch it.'

'What's she done to you?'

'Do you know what she said when I came out of the changing room?'

'What?'

'Lucky this is a jumbo jet.'

'She's just jealous.'

'I'll give her jumbo jet.'

'Don't do anything silly.'

'I won't. It's a law of the jungle that even monkeys have to have a snooze and then they get off their guard and then I'll strike.'

'Kate, I've told you to stop drinking so much. It is becoming embarrassing.'

'That little pygmy is going to pay for that, you mark my words.'

We spend the day learning about how British-American Airlines do things, which isn't so much different from the way other airlines we have worked for, except perhaps a bit more efficiently than some. But for these promotional trips they always roll out the red carpet. Even as we stand there listening to CJ's right hand man talk, they are loading the caviare, champagne, smoked salmon, and pre-cooked fillet steaks in.

'This is a very important trip for us, girls, the opening of a new route – a first for this airline I might add and a real boost for British prestige, not to mention our new plane, the Tri-Star. So let's hope it all goes very well tomorrow.'

It all sounds a bit familiar, but Kate and I try to look bright-eyed and bushy-tailed during this spiel, as befits the Airline's Personality Girls, as they insist on calling us.

'Personality girls, you must be joking,' I hear the awful Kerry mutter, 'more like bloody short-time girls.' What was that Kate was saying about the jungle? I decide to get Kerry. So daggers-drawn, we complete our day's preparation for the voyage. The whole plane is going to be full of every sort of hanger-on, PR men, advertising executives, press, journalists and assorted dignitaries, the latter invited to lend a kind of phony respectability to the whole thing. There is an ex-cabinet minister, now known as a lush and occasional journalist, a famous architect, always game for a free handout and a couple of TV personalities of the type who chair quiz games for school children. All the important ones are going first class and the rabble – mainly company employees and their wives – tourist.

I have never been to Honolulu, which is our destination, but the whole trip is so tight – with every moment scheduled for something or other – that I am sure I can handle any queries our honoured guests may have.

The highlight of the trip is to be a party, with Hula dancers, at a famous hotel near Honolulu. In view of how things turned out, I won't give its name, except to say that it is considered to be very chic and expensive. I wouldn't argue with the last. Anyway, after training Kate and I repair to our flat. It's not so much a flat as a room we have kept on in someone else's flat, a place to go to when we haven't got anything better to do. Sometimes we go and check over the rubbish to see if there is anything we can sell – sometimes we come back there with other people's husbands when we are in a tight spot, and sometimes we just leave things there when there is nowhere else to leave them. Mostly, however, we try to stay away. Kate once suggested turning it into an indoor mushroom farm on the grounds that if dry rot, wet rot, damp rot and moist rot could grow so fast, there was no reason why we shouldn't make a fortune out of mushrooms.

Anyway, there we are, sitting on the bed feeling a bit abandoned now that Jake and friends don't seem to want to see us, and pretending that we would have had an early night anyway – what with the flight and all – when who should come slouching down the stairs, past the gas meter, turn right at the broom cupboard, mind the floorboard which isn't there, and knock on our door, but little Mike, demon lover with the wife and kids in Neasden.

'Well, stone the flaming crows, look what the cat brought in.'

Actually he's quite welcome, particularly as he is carrying what looks happily like a bottle in a piece of brown paper.

'Hello, you little beauties.'

'How the hell did you find us here.'

'Well it wasn't difficult. You girls are well-known in these parts, you know. In fact you have some of the best-known parts in town.'

'Thanks, Mike, it's been a lovely evening, sorry you couldn't stay, we have to fly in the morning you know.'

'Now don't get your knickers in a twist. Pass me that tooth mug and that paper cup and we'll have a little gargle. Don't worry, I'll drink out of the bottle. There you are. So how goes things? St Trop OK?'

He's got a certain way with him which is attractive, I have to admit.

'It was OK,' I say, 'but we were both getting over a broken heart on account of you.'

'All right, let's cut out that sort of thing. I am sorry, but I know you two weren't as innocent as you pretend. You didn't fool me for a moment with all that "Kate will be back in an hour" stuff. Here have another drink.'

We pass a few pleasant minutes chatting. Mike begins to look a little distressed and eyes the place with distaste.

'Look, I don't want to put down your lovely homely little abode, but how about going somewhere where there's some oxygen in the air? Christ if I had known you lived down a coal mine I would have brought a gas mask. Come on let's nip round the pub. There is something I've got to tell you anyway.'

We practically fall over each other in our haste to get out of the place.

'Well if it's something important, I suppose we could just about slip out for a quick little drinkie, couldn't we Kate?'

Kate is already half-way up the stairs.

'OK, smooth-talker, what is it you have to tell us?' We are sitting happily in a booth in the local, large Cinzanos in front of us. Talk about the bright lights taste, this place is lit by four neon tubes. As someone once remarked, if it weren't a bloody pub you wouldn't come near it. Anything is preferable to that room amongst the growing mushrooms, though.

'OK Mike, let's have the good news.'

He is enjoying his moment. We are twitching with eagerness to hear what he has to tell us.

'Well, it's like this. Your friends Jake and Dave are under investigation by the drug squad for importing certain substances into this country in film cans. I only got out of it because Jake told the fuzz I had no idea they were doing it, which is true.'

'Oh my God. But they're not in jail or anything?'

'No, they're out on bail until their case comes up in four

weeks. They first found out they were being investigated just before we went off to Paris.'

My first reaction is relief – it explains so much about Jake's behaviour. But then I feel disappointment. Jake can't need the money, and he's too big to get involved in something like this for the fun of it.

'Why did they do it?'

'It's Dave, really. He's got a hell of a lot of debts, lives like a millionaire, and he's borrowed money from Jake already, that he hit on this way of making a little money. They put the dope in the film cans along with the real cans of unexposed film whenever they came back from aboard. Dave made a fortune. But he spent that too. So all he's got for his troubles is a spell in the nick.'

'That's so unfair, I mean Jake shouldn't go down as well.'

'It's no good saying it's unfair, Penny, Jake shouldn't have got mixed up in it.'

'Well, he was obviously trying to help a friend.'

'Sure, but if you think helping a friend import drugs into this country is smart, then there's no hope for you.'

I can see all that, but my heart goes out to Jake. I now realise why he has been so distant. Worry. It must have been hell, knowing you were going to be charged when you got back from Paris. And I deserted him.

'Look, Mike, what do you think is going to happen to them?'

'I don't know. I imagine they will get about a year or even more. It's all wrapped up.'

'Good God, a year.'

What can I do to help? Nothing it seems. Tomorrow we fly to Hawaii for four days, then we are going to see him and Dave to prepare for the rest of our filming. If they still want to do it with Jake and Dave, which is unlikely I would have thought.

'Now Penny, don't do anything stupid,' says Kate when we get back to our room for some beauty sleep before the morning's excitement. We also have to take our revenge on the ghastly Kerry and Mandy.

'What could I do to help?'

'Nothing.'

'How can you say nothing so finally?'

'Nothing, unless you want to bake them a pie with a file in it.'

'Ha, bloody ha. Quite apart from anything else, our livelihood is at stake.'

'I don't think so. After all we weren't mixed up in it at all and anyway we're employed by CJ on the airline in theory, not by Jake or the advertising agency.'

'I dare say there are a few worried faces at Nutley, Bratwurst and Cutlet at the moment.'

I lie there, feeling quite sick really. There is a lot of the romantic in me somewhere and I do feel as though I have let Jake down badly by skiving off to St Tropez in his hour of need. Still I also feel a little hurt because Jake did not confide in me. As I lie there pondering, Kate begins to undress.

I look up to see her impressive frame, clad only in the tiniest pair of red panties gyrating in front of the mirror. Her hips are going round and round and her boobs are trying to keep up.

'What are you doing, you idiot?'

'I am practising the hula hula for those balmy nights under the pacific moon.'

'You won't be doing the hula.'

'How do you know?'

'Knowing you the closest you'll come is lying on your back with someone doing it on top of you.'

'My we are in a good mood. I hope they lock you up too.'

'Aloha to you. Goodnight.'

CHAPTER TEN

'Some of us have work to do, you know.'

It's the lovely Mandy, as she minces off to the plane. Kate and I are surrounded by photographers, two actually, sent by the airline's PR Agency to photograph the momentous occasion.

We have spent the morning in Vital's getting the full treatment – face, hair, manicure – and we feel pretty terrific. The other girls just had their ordinary morning routine, and here we are getting the star treatment. Little wonder that they are a bit shirty. Still, as I tell myself, and Kate for that matter, it's not our fault. If they want to make a fight of it, let them try. I am confident Kate and I can handle it. While the other girls are in the plane getting it ready, we pose by the door, we pose with a bottle of champagne in hand, we pose at the top of the steps up to the plane, we pose everywhere.

Finally the guests begin to arrive and we have to start the real work. Kate and I greet them at the door, try to learn the names of the important ones fast, and show them to their seats in the front of the plane. The mere employees of the airline have different coloured cards on their lapels and we all but ignore them. That's show business.

All the normal rules about drinking before take-off are in abeyance today and we are soon sluicing out the champers merrily. We are boosting British prestige, so we have been told, and I find there is no better way to boost prestige than to serve up a few long drinks. This lot are cadgers and spongers, so it's a bit like trying to feed the five thousand with only two sprats, but then, He did not have ten cases of Mumm Cordon Rouge champagne on Him at the time. We do. By the time the plane takes off, not more than ten minutes have elapsed, yet our forty celebrities have managed to polish off twenty bottles of bubbly. Over in the second class section, deck passage Kate calls them, there is a tremendous cheer from the employees as the plane lifts off. Is this encouraging? Were they expecting it NOT to lift off? Who can tell? Perhaps they are finding out that champagne, even non-vintage, is stronger than Wincarnis.

Kate goes off to get the first class canapes, while I chat to a TV Personality. (I like that bit. 'What do you do for a living?' 'I am a Personality!') Suddenly there is a scream and a crash. I hasten off to see what has befallen Kate. The smoked salmon, tastefully arranged on little rounds of brown bread, snuggling up to cubes of bread with caviare heaped generously upon them, is now on the floor, a shambles. I have never seen Kate do that before in all the time we have flown together. For a big girl she is amazingly nimble.

'What happened?'
'The little bitch.'
'What happened?'
'When I opened the cupboard to get the tray out, a mouse leaped out.'
'A mouse?'
'Well, a bloody toy mouse with a spring in it. It jumped right into my face, squeaking.'
'It's those cows next door in steerage.'
'Jealously will get them nowhere. We'll fix them.'

Before we can do this we have to fix some sort of snacks

for our friends up front. I take the booze around again while Kate scrapes off the floor whatever is salvageable.

By the time she gets round, I have been so generous with the drinks that a lot of people think caviare and smoked salmon purée with wilted lettuce, is a new speciality. Out of little disasters some of the greatest dishes in the world have been created. I mean to say, roast pork was only discovered when the house burnt down taking the pigs with it, or so the story goes. That's what comes of doing 'O' level History.

We hardly have time to plan our revenge we are so busy dishing out the grub and the drink on the first leg to Chicago. But a plan begins to hatch itself in my devious little mind as we fasten our seat-belts for landing at Chicago Airport. I let it ferment for a while while we are refuelling and taking on supplies of essentials. Actually, we have another stop scheduled in Los Angeles before setting out over the Pacific, another 2,000 miles, so there is a lot of time to work out a particularly unpleasant fate for those little bitches. They prove, if proof is needed, that they really don't like us at all.

'Everything going OK?' asks Kerry with a sweet smile. 'Not out of practice, are we? Not too much of the high-life?' she says nastily. Oh, it is going to be a pleasure to give her her come-uppance.

As we set off for LA, we have a chance to get to know some of the passengers. They are all very friendly except for the TV personality who obviously has an inflated idea of his own importance. He seems to think the whole thing is a great bore and I feel like asking him why he took up the offer. You would think that being the chairman of a children's quiz show was a training for the post of God the way he waves us away languidly when we offer him anything.

'Can't you see I am trying to read?'

'Very sorry, sir.'

The one I like best is a comedian who sits absolutely poker-faced through take-off, then he grabs my hand and says 'Mummy?' His timing is superb – one of those people who is obviously genuinely funny at all times, not just when he has to read a script. I have to confess to him that I have only seen him on the telly once, but he doesn't care about that at all.

'What are you doing on this flight?' I ask him.

'Shhh. I think they sent the ticket to the wrong feller. Don't let on, they may ask me to jump out.'

He makes friends with all the other passengers, and by the time we come to serve dinner he has most of them weak with laughter. I know nothing about golf, but the way he describes it is hilarious. And he can do hundreds of accents. It is amazing, even the pearls and twinset wife of an architect wants him to say 'You are awful, but I like you'.

'That's Dick Emery, not me.'

'Well do it anyway.'

He has me in stitches all the way to LA. Because of the time lag, we still have an hour of daylight left. But on the last leg to Honolulu most of the passengers sleep soundly. The only one in our section who stays awake is a journalist who has an insatiable appetite for Scotch, which he drinks straight without any ice or water. He has not left the first class bar since we took off and he is beginning to show it.

'You have to drink a lot in a plane. Bloody air is de-hydrated by the engines, that's why you have to drink so much, see. Cheers.'

'Don't you want to get some sleep, sir?'

'Sleep? Never touch it myself. Bad for the kidneys.'

He makes a bit of a lurch for me and instead of patting me affectionately on the shoulder, gets me right on the boob.

'Terribly sorry, love. Didn't mean to. Nice though.' He slumps down on a seat near the bar, glass in hand.

He begins to mumble about the five-mile-high club, which all male passengers aspire to join after a few drinks.

'I am already a member, sir,' I say, fending him off, 'but I know a girl who is dying to join.'

I get one of the stewards to tell Kerry that there is a journalist in the bar who wants to interview one of the real stewardesses.

'You give her this when she comes, OK?' I mix a huge drink, vodka, gin and brandy, heavily laced with orange liqueur to disguise it. I give him a wink. 'Pretend you want to interview her, OK, and don't take no for an answer? She's dying to join. I will see you are not disturbed.'

As I am busying myself near the galley, Kerry comes by looking smug.

'Where are you going?'

'You're not the only one on the plane the journalists want to know about, you know. I am being interviewed by the *Barnsley Clarion*!'

'Oh, good for you.' She is slightly tipsy already.

The rest of the plane is in near darkness by now. I watch Kerry going up the stairs to the bar with glee. Kate thinks it is the funniest thing since toothache.

'Anyway, she might have a good time. Why didn't you send me up there?'

'I'll get the steward to go up in half an hour and look for her. Then we'll see.'

Despite her doubts, Kate can't wait to have a look.

'Give them a chance, I mean she's got to drink that drink still.'

But I am dying to see how they are getting on too. I creep up the stairs after ten minutes and peek up.

There on the floor of the first-class bar is a sight I would not want to miss. Kerry has her uniform, or what's left of it, hanging loosely round her ankles. There seems to be a lot of confusion. Our journalist is trying to get on top of her, but his trouser legs are twisted round his ankles. It looks like the sack race at the paraplegics olympics. I feel rather sorry for Kerry, because she is beginning to moan, and it's not sexual ecstasy. If I am any judge of these matters, we shall be seeing her impromptu Hawaiian punch make a sudden reappearance. The journalist finally gets his trousers off, over his shoes. He is now wearing only a tie and his shoes and socks. Even if he can get Kerry facing in the right direction, she has now turned over, and curled under a chair, he is going to have a lot of bother getting it together from what I can see of him. Talk about limp, this is like a piece of wet macaroni. I watch fascinated as he drags her out by the legs from under the table, and tries to turn her face up. But discretion is the better part of valour, so I leave before Kerry, virtually unconscious, joins the club. Actually, as I have said, it will only be a technical membership as there seems little chance of anything being consummated, which is rule one, page one, of the members' handbook.

Kate calls the steward and tells him he had better go and sort out what's going on in his bar. By the time he gets there it is too late. They have subsided in a drunken heap, the punch is seeping into the carpet and their clothes are strewn all over the bar. Lucy and Mandy are summoned to take their colleague to a lavatory as discreetly as possible, and two stewards straighten up the journalist as best they can with wet towels and black coffee. Poor Kerry can hardly walk. As she comes by us, Kate says,

'What happened? Couldn't she handle the high life?'

'Are you sure we haven't gone too far?'

'No. Everyone will want to hush this one up.'

She's quite right, as it turns out. The PR man from British-American calls me in with the Captain, and we all agree it would be best to say nothing about it at all. Pretend it never happened. Stum, all that sort of thing.

'Personally I think it is disgraceful, Captain, but if you feel that's the way we should handle it, you can rely on me.'

'That's the idea Penny. I mean this is a special flight and he is an important journalist. Quite a lot of people read the *Barnsley Clarion*.'

'Particularly in Barnsley.'

'Quite.'

After the PR man has gone, the Captain, who is about forty, very RAF with his moustache and black hair, says: 'I have a pretty shrewd idea what happened. Maybe she deserved it, but don't get too carried away with your success.'

'Yessir.'

'OK, run along now.' He gives me a shrewd pinch as I go. Must watch him obviously. Too clever by half, and quite good looking in a Biggles sort of way. He's probably a founder member of the five-mile-high club.

I summon Lucy and Mandy. 'Now I have just had a word with the Captain, and he has agreed to overlook this behaviour this once owing to the special circumstances of this trip. But he has asked me to tell you to impress upon Kerry, when she returns to the land of the living, that this sort of thing cannot be tolerated on an international airline. Do you understand?'

The cat seems to have got their tongues.

'I am assuming of course, that you two don't carry on in this fashion in flight, but nonetheless Captain Squires asked me to pass on his warning to you two as well.'

By the time we land in Honolulu, Kerry has revived enough to attempt to sing. Lucy and Mandy put her under a blanket at the back of the plane and tell the passengers that she has food poisoning. It's a good try. But as she breaks into Yellow Submarine, she gets some very funny looks.

It is early evening in Honolulu. The air is warm and fragrant, like the inside of a florist's shop.

'Game set and match,' says Kate. 'I think we are going to enjoy it here.'

The flash bulbs pop, a team of Hawaiian dancers begin to undulate on the tarmac and all the passengers are garlanded with leis. The sound of the Hawaiian guitar and Sweet Leilani contrast strangely with the fainter, but nonetheless brave, rendition of Yellow Submarine coming from somewhere inside the plane. A wheelchair arrives to take away the fearless campaigner of the *Barnsley Clarion*. He appears to have a severe case of food poisoning too. You can tell by the way he keeps unzipping his trousers that he's worried about it.

CHAPTER ELEVEN

Hawaii is a treat. We go that evening straight to our Hotel, which is a little way outside Honolulu, set on a beautiful lagoon. Although it is now after midnight London time, nobody wants to go to bed. Except perhaps the wretched Kerry. It's magical being transported from London to the middle of the Pacific in a day. A traditional Hawaiian feast has been laid on for us in a replica of a long house in Polynesian style in the grounds of our hotel. Despite all our travelling all over the world, Kate and I are very excited as we change out of our uniforms.

'What should I wear?'

'Your grass skirt?'

'Funny, aren't you?'

'How about just those leis around your top.'

'Yes I would like a lay.'

'Kate, (a) that is very crude and (b) that is what's known as tautology.'

'What does that mean?'

'Stating the obvious.'

After much indecision, we settle for long, simple cotton shifts from Miss Selfridge. Kate has an oatmeal coloured one and mine is brown. They were made for the slighter figure really, but they look pretty sensational on us. In Kate's case it's a touch obscene at the top, but she puts her lei round her neck to give it a semblance of decency.

'I feel like some adventure tonight.'

'So do I. Men of Hawaii and the Western Pacific, you are warned.'

We stroll across the grass which flows down to the lagoon. Giant palms are dotted about the landscape, each one lit by spotlights. The long house is thatched on top but completely open to the winds from the sea on the sides. And it is very long. Traditionally whole families and even whole tribes used to occupy one house, some of which would be fortified against invaders. This one is a replica of the less warlike long houses, open for coolness. In the middle of the house is a dug-out canoe, full of punch, which everyone drinks, through a straw, out of half a coconut shell, probably not the original Polynesian way of drinking it, but very good for all that. It is white and milky with bits of fruit floating in it. Fantastic.

Outside the long house in a trench, they are roasting suckling pigs. The process, so Captain Squires tells me, for he has been here before, is to cover the pig in mud and bake it for six hours. You then break open the mud, scrape off the ash, and have a succulent, tender suckling pig.

'It's the traditional Polynesian way of cooking. Not recommended for bedsitters in Earls Court, ha, ha.'

He obviously thinks it's a pretty good joke, because I hear him telling it to Kate a moment later. She stares at him wide-eyed.

'No? Why not?'

'Well, you would have to dig a trench in the floor.'

'Oh, I see. You are clever.'

'Come with me and have another punch.'

Off we go. He's jolly dapper, our skipper, chatting up the ladies, telling jokes, passing out helpful bits of information free of charge; in fact generally being quite unbearable. I try to get away but he keeps leading us off to meet people, firmly grasping my arm.

Fortunately when the food is ready, there is such a commotion, what with everybody wanting to see the suckling pigs being dug up, a bit like Tutankhamen, as Kate points out, that we manage to evade him. I feel he might try to use his authority to blackmail me a bit into something I might not like. He has tumbled to our little joke with Kerry and I am sure he intends to use the information.

The suckling pig is delicious. And some of the local men are delicious too. A whole party of them in warpaint suddenly come skimming over the water, beach their outrigger canoe and race into the hut. They do a very dramatic war dance, lots of sweating brown bodies and grass skirts. They point their paddles at us in a menacing fashion, shout and chant and then leap back into the canoe, and are gone into the night.

'Just like those men at the beginning of Hawaii Five-O,' I say.

'Probably got another couple of hotels to do before their tea,' says the comedian Ed. He is so smothered in leis that he looks like the cenotaph on Memorial Day. He is showing some interest in one of the waitresses, a lovely Chinese girl, but he is not getting anywhere, so he tells us.

'Now in Britain every waitress in the country knows me. But here nobody has ever heard of me or my show. Very challenging.' He laughs wickedly. You can't help liking the man.

The people of Hawaii are a great mixture of races, from the original Polynesians to the Chinese and Japanese who have settled over the years. They speak with broad American accents, which surprises me at first, but then even if they don't look like it, they are Americans. Everyone tells me, in that irritating way people have who have been somewhere before, that the other islands are much more beautiful, and not nearly so commercialized. But this looks OK to me. Tomorrow we are going to see the Haleakala

Volcano and have lunch on a little island near by. So we shall see for ourselves.

The party of welcome is dying a death because everyone is so tired after the flight. Only our indefatigable skipper is still smiling away, even though it's now 4.00 am London time. As people begin to drift off to bed, he suggests a little nightcap to me in his room. I don't want to go – I mean if I am going to have to wrestle it would be far nicer with one of the locals, but he says that we need to talk about business.

'All right, but not too long, I am very tired.'

'When I was in the Air Force we used to go on missions and not get any sleep at all for thirty-six hours. Part of the training. Never got out of the habit.'

'Yes, well, I was in the Army, so I wouldn't know about that sort of thing.'

'Ha, ha, jolly funny.' He has a sort of bark when he laughs which makes his Biggles moustache quiver. He puts a friendly, all too friendly, arm around me as we head back to his room. Am I imagining it, or is his hand creeping down over my shoulder on to my boob? I am not imagining it. His fingers find their way into my bodice and begin to massage one of my breasts vigorously.

'Now, now, Skipper, I thought this was business.'

'It is, my dear it is, but there it has always been my belief that a chap should mix business and pleasure, wherever possible.'

'Well if a chap would take his hand out of my dress, perhaps you could tell me what you want to discuss.'

'Come inside and have a drink and I'll tell you.'

Can he be that unsubtle that he really wants to lure me in before pouncing? He can. He does. As soon as we get inside the door, he is on me like a barrel of monkeys. Now Penny, I say to myself, this is where you take a moral stand.

But there isn't a lot of time for moral stands. He has undone the top of my shift and is burying his moustache between my breasts and burrowing like a furry mole. Suddenly he comes up for air.

'I am a tit man myself.' And he's gone again.

'You had me fooled for a moment. I thought you were a foot fetishist who had missed the turning.'

I hear a muffled ha, ha. His moustache quivers and tickles me.

'Now look here, Skipper, do you have anything you want to say?'

'Yes, get your knickers off.'

His furry face moves down my body. I try to speak to him and stop him, but he's unstoppable. In no time at all he has me stripped like a banana on the bed. I clutch at my briefs, but he just burrows away. I feel as though I am being assaulted by a demented koala bear. He simply takes no notice when I try to stop him pulling off my panties.

'This will tickle your fancy,' he says. It does. Actually, being a sensible sort of girl, I have realized that protest is useless, and I might as well enjoy it. His moustache and his head disappear between my legs, and soon my body is quivering with sensations. Some of them very strange indeed.

'You still a tit man, Skipper?' I manage to inquire between gasps.

'No, I've changed my allegiance.' His voice is a little muffled, but I see what he means. Actually his probing tongue and his moustache practically drive me crazy. I am half laughing and half screaming. It's like being tickled to death. By the time he comes up and moves on top of me I am quite exhausted. He is very brisk and efficient in his love-making, too. I lie on the bed practically unconscious, but he gets up, pours a drink for us, and begins to sing. He is a strange one, this. So much energy. In no time at all he is running his furry face over my breasts again, but I just can't stand any more. And anyway it's 5.00 am London time.

'Must go now, Skipper, see you.' I start pulling on my clothes as fast as I can.

'OK, well give me a ring before brekkers if you feel like another bombing run.'

'I see, then you'll tell me about the business we have to discuss.'

'That's the ticket, bottoms up, wizard prang that, eh?'

'Well goodnight, I must go back to my hangar.'

'Ha, ha,' his moustache practically rotates it is so amused.

'Back to your hangar, ha, ha banzai, jolly good bash. See you in the morning old girl.'

I feel a bit like an old girl after the Captain's Kamikaze raid on me. I know it seems awful, but really what could I do to avoid it? You can't tell the captain to piss off, in my experience – you have to be subtle about it, like talking about your fiancé, but old Biggles here won't take no for an answer.

I run into Kate creeping down the corridor to our room as well.

'Hello old girl, have a wizard bash did you, splendid, jolly good show, eh what?'

'Penny Sutton, are you OK? Not drunk too much Hawaiian punch have you?' She sounds genuinely concerned.

I tell her the story of my evening as we undress for bed.

'Sounds as though you distinguished yourself in action, Penelope, here let me award you the DFC. Distinguished F. . .ing Cross.'

'And what have you been up to, my little sprite? Playing canasta?'

She looks a little rough too, poor thing. As though a rugby team has passed over her without stopping.

'Well, it was like this, I met the rowing eight, you know the ones in the grass skirts who came over the waves, a bit later and they sort of showed me a good time.'

'All eight of them?'

'Good God, what do you think I am, a masochist?'

'Yes.'

'Just one of them. The good-looking one.'

'The cox?'

'Of course he had . . . oh I see what you mean. Actually, now you mention it, it was quite the biggest whatsit I've ever seen.'

'Where did you meet him, in his hut?'

'Hut, hell. After the show they all drive home in Cadillacs. There's good business in paddling your own canoe. We went back to his beach house.'

'It must have been a bit sexy with all that grass skirt bit.'

'He wore a white tuxedo in the discotheque, which is where I met them, and is a college graduate. You must meet him and his friends, they are fun.'

'Tell you what, I'll do you a trade, Biggles for your cox with the big cox.'

'Kind of you to offer, but no thanks. What are you going to do with Captain Squires, anyway?'

'I don't know. We can't afford to antagonize him, can we? A bad report from him and we'll be out. But if you think I am going to go on a bombing raid with him every night, you're crazy.'

'I never suggested anything of the sort, Penny, but now you come to mention it, it would be bad policy to antagonize him. Well, I mean it's only a few days.' She laughs wickedly as she falls asleep. I am so tired I cannot argue or even think about my predicament and off I go to the land of nod without another thought. If nothing else, Biggles is a good sleeping pill. I don't even have time to ask myself how I get into these situations. Which is perhaps fortunate. I might not like the answer.

We catch up for lost sleep because, of course, we get the benefit of the extra hours. We 'Personality Girls' have a photo call after breakfast by the swimming pool in our bikinis. It has to be quick because the boat for Haleakala Volcano, specially chartered of course, leaves from the harbour at 11.00 am. We lounge around the pool and the photographers from the local papers, not to mention British-American's PR Agency, snap us. They seem keen to get as much cleavage as possible, so we oblige, because we're keen to get off and away and anyway we're obliging by nature. Twice I slip down the top of my bikini until my nipples are practically out before they are satisfied. Still, if it's good publicity for the airline and for us we'll do it. And worse.

Half an hour later we jump in a taxi and tell the driver to step on it down to the harbour, which is a good few miles away. He obliges, but we get pulled over by a police car. They have obviously all been watching Hawaii Five-O around here. And this one fancies himself as McGarrett.

'Well where would you be going in such a hurry, mister?'

The taxi driver is no mug. 'Well, Chief,' he says, 'these two beautiful young ladies from England are movie stars from England, and they are promoting our beautiful islands, islands of a thousand different faces, in England, and they are late for their specially chartered boat to Haleakala, to be photographed in that renowned beauty spot, for showing in England.'

'OK feller, I am as patriotic as the next guy. You follow me. And you're in trouble if you can't keep up.'

Gun bulging at his hip, he runs for his police car, turns on the lights and the siren and heads for the harbour at ninety miles an hour. I can see him now, chewing gum, his jaw jutting out almost as far as his belly, his eyes like burnished steel behind the dark glasses, scattering pedestrians and tourists alike as we speed away. Or have I been watching too much Hawaii Five-O too? It's an infectious complaint in these parts.

CHAPTER TWELVE

'Vesuvius makes this look like a vicarage tea-party.' It's our resident know-all, the TV personality speaking.

'Yes but Vesuvius is extinct,' says the guide pleasantly.

'That's what you think. It's due for another eruption in the next five years.'

'Well this one erupts every day.'

'How regular. Perhaps it's on All Bran.'

Indeed as we stand there we can see smoke curling from the top of the volcano, which is itself on the top of a small island. It looks a bit like an inverted ice cream cone, this island, and is practically unspoilt. There is a magnificent hotel, formerly an old colonial mansion, where we dock the boat. After a few refreshing drinks – this is worrying, we seem to be drinking morning, noon and night – we pile into jeeps and make the trip up to the volcano. It's a bit daft, isn't it? You would think the last thing you would do is try and climb into a volcano, rather like attending your own cremation, but anyway, that's what the man says – we are going to go into the crater. We wind upwards on a track through the jungle. As we get closer I can hear the volcano rumbling, like an old man with indigestion.

'Now folks, step this way please.'

We climb some steps, to a viewing platform, and there below us is the heart of the volcano. It looks like a glowing coal fire. Smoke billows up and the surrounding landscape is covered with ash.

'She's not due to erupt for another three hours, so if you want to come any closer, follow me.'

I decline the invitation. It's hot enough here. Anyway, as Kate says, I don't want to know what hell's going to be like just yet, I'll have quite enough time to find out when I'm dead. And after old Biggles's efforts last night I don't feel too energetic. Thank God he's not with us today. The sight of his moustache might just finish me off. Our intrepid party goes down the path towards the volcano while Kate and I sit under the shade of a large rock. We are admiring the truly sensational view down to the hotel and the harbour, when we hear stealthy footsteps. It is the driver of one of the jeeps. He is a large, Polynesian looking man, dressed in a Hawaiian shirt.

'Hello,' we say.

He does not reply but begins to take off his trousers. I don't know what to do, but Kate begins to clap.

'Terrific. Give us a flash.'

Solemnly he stands in front of us with his trousers round his ankles and this enormous thing pointing skywards like a guided missile. Perhaps if I press the button it will go off.

'Lovely, what do you do for an encore?' Kate finds the whole thing terribly amusing. I simply can't believe the size of his old man. I am not a great admirer of this part of the male equipment, but this one is the size of a prize-winning marrow. Perhaps he is so pleased with himself he simply had to show us.

'Great, a Royal Command Performance,' says Kate cheerily.

Without so much as a flicker of emotion, he begins to button himself up and turns and goes back to the jeep.

'Kate, I think it may be a fertility rite. This volcano is sacred to the Hawaiians.'

'I think he's a flasher.'

'Sherlock Goodbody. Scotland Yard have vacancies for people like you.'

'See what I mean about these Polynesians.'

'What?'

'Remember what I told you about that cox with the big . . .'

'Yes, yes. Do you think it's a national characteristic?'

'Well we can live in hope.'

'Tell you what, let's have a competition to see who can find the biggest in Hawaii.'

'But we're only here for three days more.'

'We'll have to work fast.'

'How are we going to tell who the winner is?'

'That's a good point. You can't exactly bring out a tape measure at the crucial moment.'

'No, and we'll be hard put to improve on our friend over there.'

'I mean it has to be in the field of action. It's no good just flashers and the like popping up.'

'I'll tell you what, we'll have to be truthful. Compare at the end of the trip.'

'OK, it's a deal.'

'What's the prize?'

'The loser takes Biggles to the Hammersmith Pally for a lovely evening's dancing.'

'Anything but that. What about the winner nominating a forfeit for the loser.'

'OK.'

The bargain is struck. The rest of our party reappear, looking a bit red in the face. The quest for the Greater Polynesian Male Member is on.

At lunch in the hotel I begin to size up, if you'll forgive expression, likely contenders. We go down to the beach for a laze about and some more of the ever-present punch, and I spot a beach boy who looks like he might be a runner. Actually it has never been one of my talents setting out to pick up men, it usually happens the other way round, but a bet is a bet, I always say. At least I am saying it now. He is a magnificent piece of beefsteak, about twenty years old, dark curly hair, broad brown shoulders. How to get him into a position where I can compete, that's the problem. I ask him to take me out in the hotel's speedboat to see the reef about two or three hundred yards off the shore. The punch has made me slightly woozy anyway, so I give Kate a cheery wave as we set off over the blue waters. I lie back on the upholstered seat, undo the strap of my bikini and soak up the sun. My pilot's broad, brown back is all I can see as we fly over the waves.

The surprise on his face as he cuts the motor and turns to show me the sights, is a pleasure I miss, because I have my eyes shut as though dozing in the sun. The bikini has slipped three quarters of the way off my boobs. From behind my dark glasses I survey the front of his trunks for any tell-tale signs of life. Nothing. He must be made of ice.

'Wonderful out here,' I say, 'so far from the madding crowd.'

Perhaps he does not appreciate English poetry, because he does not reply.

'What's your name?'

'Joe.'

'Well it's nice to know you Joe. How's business in the beach boy trade union at the moment?'

'Not bad.'

My bikini top has now slipped right down. I take it off and turn face down.

'Do you mind, Joe?'

'Hell no, you go right ahead.'

This is a bit slick for a beach boy on a near-uninhabited Polynesian island, I tell myself. Perhaps he is the son of the owner of the place.

I decide to have a swim, topless, and see how he reacts.

He does not at all. Sutton, you're slipping. He seems more interested in looking at himself in a mirror he has conveniently placed in the cockpit than at the untramelled Penelope Sutton floating seductively in the clear water. I come to the edge of the boat, peer at him appealingly, and say, 'Help me out of the water Joe.'

'Sure. Here put your foot on the ladder, that's it.'

Even contact with my wet, sexy flesh doesn't seem to stir him. Oh well you can't win them all, I am saying to myself mentally, as I dry and lie down on my back.

'Do you do this all year round?'

'My goodness, what ever gave you that idea? No I am a drama student in LA. This is a vacation job. Well a boy's got to do something to keep himself in mink during the winter.'

Oh my god. A queer, Polynesian beach boy. It can't be true. It is. Joe's greatest ambition, it turns out, is to do Iago to one of our great theatrical knights' Othello. I don't like to point out to him that his delicate brown colour is perhaps more suited to the role of Othello, but I must say he is quite charming really. He has that obsessive self-interest that keeps actors going when other mortals would give it all up to become milkmen. Once we start talking about him, there is no stopping him. I tell him about our bet, and he laughs uproariously. It is his idea to fool Kate, so we hatch our little scheme. We are both close to tears at the prospect of it by the time we get back to the beach. As I get off the boat I give him a little peck on the cheek, he tries to look butch, and I stroll, smirking, up to Kate. At first I don't say anything to her, just keep on smiling.

'How did you get on?'

'Terrific.' I stretch like a cat that's had the cream.

'I mean in our competition.'

'Not bad.'

'What are you trying to hold out on me, Penny Sutton?'

'Darling, this was a new experience, I am still bathed in the after-glow.'

'You'll be bathed in the rest of my bloody rum punch if you don't tell me about it.'

'Now, now don't get shirty. This was one of the great romantic experiences of my life. I don't want to debase it by talking about it.'

'Oh rubbish. When did you get so discreet? Kiss-and-tell Sutton is your name.'

'This is special, something different.'

'What's your game Penny?'

'Look, Kate,' I draw her aside and begin to whisper, although the nearest body is fifteen yards away. 'Look, this boy is not just large, I think he must have had an elephant's trunk grafted on.'

'Really? I wonder what it is that makes them like this. Perhaps it's the coconut oil.'

'Honestly, I can't believe this isn't the winner outright.'

'Come on, there's only been my bloke. You can hardly call Biggles a Polynesian.'

'Or a contender for that matter. More like a randy tea cosy than anything.'

I let it sink in for a while. Then I have an idea.

'Tell you what Kate, Joe, that's him, is going to Honolulu tonight, so I'll invite him to a party at the hotel, then we can swap, I'll have your cox, and we can decide who's the winner.'

'My, forward, aren't we? And who says I'm interested in that muscle-bound teenager?'

'He's twenty. I think.'

'Well maybe.' I can tell she's more than interested.

We lie on the beach roasting gently for an hour or so.

'My, my, look what the cat brought in.'

It's Kerry, Mandy and Lucy, the terrible trio, coming up the beach towards us. They have been avoiding us since we got to Hawaii. And with good reason. They know when they are defeated. Trouble is they don't.

'Hear you and the skipper are getting on well,' says Mandy pointedly.

'Yes, we were discussing your friend's performance in the first class bar. Captain Squires and I were wondering whether or not to put it in our report on the trip.'

'And what did you decide?'

'We decided to wait and see how she behaved on the way home.'

'All this in his room in the wee hours? Ha.' She snorts.

'Why don't you go for a swim,' says Kate, 'I believe there are some sharks just out there.'

They stroll off, trying to look superior, but their white English bodies let them down a bit. Actually Lucy is a bright shade of pink, but it nearly matches her hair so that's OK as colour schemes go.

I must say, the airline have excelled themselves for our party in Honolulu. There is a waterfall in the garden, set in a mock ravine, all lit by coloured lights. We drink even more of the lovely, powerful punch – and the sun has no sooner gone down than the moon appears, like a prop from the Christmas pantomime. Also like something from the Christmas pantomime, Prince Charming himself, comes Captain Squires, him of the large, tickly moustache. He gives me a concealed squeeze, somewhere in the nether regions, and I give him a kick on the ankle.

'Had a lovely day, darling?'

'Lovely, thank you Captain. Didn't miss you a bit.'

'Ha, ha.' He can't believe this for a moment. His moustache twirls.

'Lovely evening, must do my social duty, eh, see you a bit later for a bit of the old one two, eh?'

'Not a chance,' I say under my breath. 'Bigger fish to fry.' Bigger eels to fry is what I am thinking, but that's not for him to know.

The gay Polynesian drama student, part-time beach boy and lover of theatrical knights appears. My God, he looks like a tuti frutti ice cream. Pink satin suit, green lace shirt open to the waist, and white shoes. His hair is teased up into a great bouffant, like my older sister's used to be when she went bopping at the Lyceum.

'Jesus, Joe, you look a bit camp.'

'Don't worry, darling, you should see me when I dress up.'

We dance a bit until I get a sight of Kate with her feller. He is about six feet tall, very good-looking, wearing a blue blazer and white trousers. Compared to Joe, his dress looks positively funereal. Then we all sit down for a drink, and do the mutual introductions. Joe is terribly good at acting butch, though I suspect he fancies Kate's feller, Duane, even more than I do. And that's a lot. He has the most beautiful eyes, and after Kate's desciptions of his other assets, I can't wait to get at him.

Unfortunately for my ambitions, the hula hula dancing intervenes. Fifty or so young girls in grass skirts materialize from behind the grotto, two blokes with conch shells appear on top of the waterfall, and assorted musicians pop out from behind the foliage. For half an hour they play and dance the hypnotic rhythms of the Western Pacific. After quarter of an hour I wish they would shut up. Perhaps it is a bit over-commercialized, but that sickly sweet Hawaiian music gets right up my bracket. Still, for the men in the party the grass skirt-swishing bit is quite exciting. A few fairly obvious jokes about lawn mowers fly about, particularly from Ed, who is completely entranced by the whole spectacle. I suspect, though, that he sees it as material for a sketch.

It's quite late before I can get to grips with Duane. He asks me for a dance, and as I nestle against him, I see that Joe is working nicely. He and Kate are glued together. For a horrible moment I suspect that he is not gay after all. There is a look on Kate's face as we pass each other that suggests she may have found the elixir of life. That will be the cucumber Joe has put in his trousers for the occasion. He gives me a broad wink. Kate actually looks a bit apprehensive. She draws me aside for a moment.

'It can't be true. Can it?'

'It can. You better go and find out.'

After a while she and Joe slip off. I feel something stirring in Duane's trousers. My God. It's certainly not a cucumber, because it's moving. A courgette today, a cucumber tomorrow. I press myself against him.

'Do you want to come down to my beach house for a night-cap?'

I am half-way into his Cadillac before he can change his mind. The thought of Kate's rage spurs me on quite as much as my keenness to see the legendary weapon.

Modesty almost prevents me from describing what comes next. But I know my readers will want to know. In the interests of your next package holiday, ladies, may I recommend you try Hawaii. I really cannot believe the size of the thing when we are lying near naked on his bed. I have the most outrageous desire to take a picture of it, the way big game hunters do after they have shot an elephant, to decorate my wall back in London. He kisses my breasts, and begins to stroke me all over. I let my hand slip rather timidly down to his belly. I feel quite inadequate to the task. It's about the size of a baby's arm. Suddenly I get a bit nervous: although I am quite ready, I wonder if it will work.

He lowers me on to it gently, and as I begin to move, to my amazement it seems to find most of its way inside me. He is very considerate, almost too considerate, so after a while I slip on to my back and pull him on top of me. I feel as though he is trying to fill me from head to toe. As tears begin to come to my eyes, he stops and looks at me tenderly.

'Don't stop, oh don't stop now.'

CHAPTER THIRTEEN

Kate is not cool towards me in the morning. On the contrary, she is absolutely icy.

'What a pathetic little trick. How like you. How mean, petty and underhand.'

'And funny.'

'I didn't think so.'

'Not even a tiny little bit?'

'Well may be just a little.'

'Tell me what happened.'

'Well, there I was with Joe, dancing with him, and I simply could not believe the size of this thing in his trousers. We went outside, me dying to make a comparison in the interests of science, you know the feeling I am sure, and we get up against a palm tree. He won't let me undo his trousers, so finally we get back to my room. That's where I discover the cucumber. And there I am hopping around the room in my panties.'

Kate and I burst out laughing. She has to admit it was a fair cop. The only trouble is, I now have to do a forfeit of her choice because Duane is the winner on a walk-over. Anyway, the way I am feeling this morning, I don't propose to carry on my researches. It could be the death of me. Kate and I laugh weakly for a while. She is a great sport old Kate – that's why we get on so well – you can't stop her laughing for a minute. Life is far too short to go about being introverted and depressed, I think. I mean the good Lord only gave us a few years, so we might as well make the most of them. Kate and I do our humble bit to make the world a happier place. Certainly lots of men would testify to our efforts.

Talking of men, here comes bloody Biggles. His idea of holiday gear is a pair of blue shorts, rope-soled sailing shoes and a Hawaiian shirt, so bright it makes the humming birds in the trees look like sparrows in need of a spruce up.

'Hello old girl,' he says to neither of us in particular, 'how's tricks? Been getting a little of the local colour, so I hear tell.'

'Yes, we love to explore a place fully, you know mix with the people and that.'

'Personally never had a thing against your fuzzy wuzzy. Not terribly reliable sort of chap, but quite nice.'

'Is that so?'

'Oh yes. Don't want to fly with one of their airlines, damned dangerous. Still I think I would rather fly with a fuzzy airline than with the Eyties. All Spaghetti and shit!'

He wanders off, fingering his moustache, wondering perhaps if the tropical air is doing it good.

'Now young Penelope Sutton,' says our Kate, 'I think I have an idea of the forfeit you are going to have to pay me on account of how I found the feller with the biggest . . .'

'Yes, I know. Don't tell me about it. Tears come to my eyes just at the mention of it.'

'Well, what you will have to do is this. As you know, there is on our plane a little lift from the galley to the stores. I want to know if two people can have sexual congress in the stores. It could be a breakthrough like on the jumbos.'

It is a little known fact, probably because crews want to keep it secret, that there is a lift on jumbo jets. It has been known, and I am afraid yours truly is guilty, for two young people in love to take the lift down to the stores, leave the door open so it can't be summoned from above and go at each other like stoats in the rutting season. On our new plane it is only just big enough for one, and when you get down to the bottom there's standing room only between the shelves. So our Kate has set me a bit of a challenge. But a bet is a bet, as I always say, when it suits. I think this could be a new chapter in the annals of the five-mile-high club.

'You're a pal, Kate.'

'Oh yes, there's one condition.'

'Yes?' I ask suspiciously.

'You have to bring his jockey shorts back up with you as proof.'

'Kate you know me. Never one to cheat on a bet. But this is daft. I doubt if one person could get his or her knickers off down there, let alone two.'

'Well if that's how you're going to react, I suppose the whole thing is off.'

'Now, I didn't say that.'

So we agree. How do I get into these situations? A psychologist might suggest that subconsciously I like a challenge, some excitement. There is some devil that drives me on, I think. Still, with Kate around you don't need any more devils.

That day we have to work far too hard. The American PR machine is really something else. It begins to grind out a series of soppy stories about us. Here we are at Honolulu Zoo; then opening a new home for retired airline personnel; later we have another series of pictures in our bikinis at the swimming pool of a new motel which is associated with our airline. Smile, smile, smile.

'I feel like a member of the Royal Family. It must be one hell of a grind opening textile factories, laying foundation stones, and smiling your wretched head off all your life. Poor Queen. I feel quite sorry for her.

There are two photographers and they vie with each other to dream up the most idiotic angles possible. Quite a lot of them are up our skirts, which are very short. Lunch is with the Association of Travel Agents and Operators. Sounds a bit like a trade union, but it turns out they are a jolly lot. Even Hawaiians, it seems, like to travel to other parts of the world to see what's going on. They are involved in the promotion of our airline too, and so we go along to help. This means pictures with almost every one of the agents. We also sign full sized photos of ourselves for their windows. 'Hello, I'm Penny.' And there I am in living colour with Tower Bridge in the background. After lunch someone shows some films of England, during which Kate falls asleep and begins to snore delicately. I have to administer a sharp kick on the shins to shut her up.

'You're not a personality girl. More like a wardress at Belsen,' says she.

'My dear Kate. The harm you could do to Anglo-American relations by snoring during a film called "Shakespeare Country, Including Warwick Castle and a Visit to an Oxford College", is incalculable.'

'Can't we get out of this? Pretend we're ill or something? If I see another shot of Anne Hathaway's cottage I think I shall scream!'

'Now don't be temperamental. Air stewardesses should be calm, smiling and relaxed at all times. It says so in the handbook, the one you used for loo paper during the shortage.'

It's another round of coffee and biscuits, another round of tepid champagne, another round of odd little cocktail snacks on bits of toast, another round of speeches and another round of publicity photographs before we can get away. We have arranged to meet Ed, who has a hired car, for a late afternoon swim and a few frolics on the beach.

He has managed to get himself a huge, floppy hat to wear in his Mustang. The whole effect is of a flying linen bag, for he drives like a loony.

'I tell you what, if you could bottle and sell the air in this place, you could make a million. It makes me feel about ten years younger.'

The beaches close to Honolulu are very crowded normally, but at this time of the evening they are all deserted. It is magical swimming as the sun goes down over the Pacific. It is so red and round it hardly looks real. Ed, it transpires, can't actually swim too well. He makes a great pretence, but I am pretty sure one foot is on the ground. We stand in the gentle surf, the evening air getting a little chilly now and he suddenly holds our hands as we watch the last rays of the sun on the water.

'I'm glad I met you girls and I'm extra glad I came. This is beautiful.'

For a moment we stand transfixed. The awful truth that we will be back in grimy London tomorrow hits us all hard. Still, I am dying to see Jake again. Even though it's only been a week or so, I miss him a lot. It seems so unfair that he should be in trouble for helping a friend. And I do have the sense that I let him down by not understanding he was in trouble when we skived off to France. Still, every girl likes to think she is indispensable to her man. It may be vanity. Poor Jake, the thought of him in the nick breaking stones, breaks my heart.

For the moment I try not to think about it. We race up the beach to Ed's Mustang and head back to the hotel. Kate and I have to go out to the airport for a staff meeting before the return flight tomorrow. The crew are a motley collection this evening in their Hawaiian shirts, jeans, sandals and what have you. They don't look as though they could fly a kite, let alone a huge airplane. We get briefed by the captain about tomorrow's flight. The chief steward runs through the menus with us, and the captain takes up the story again.

'Now look here, it's been a wizard trip and I don't want any slips on the homeward trip. I want tight discipline. Certain incidents on the way here were not satisfactory behaviour among cabin staff, and I think you can safely say that any repetition will be met with the high jump.'

Does he mean he will open the door and make someone jump out? Could be. His moustache twirls with satisfaction as he tells us about our mission. You could just see him standing there briefing his squadron to go and drop bombs on the enemy. Did I really get involved with him? I need to pinch myself to be sure. Yes. Diminished responsibility, your worship.

'Now I want the whole crew looking bright and fresh tomorrow morning, so it's an early night for us all.'

To tell the truth, Kate and I are only too glad to comply. The system seems to be slowing down a bit under all the punishment it has taken over the last few weeks. Just time for a nightcap with Ed and one or two of his innumerable friends before bed. And a word in his ear about his jockey shorts.

The islands recede behind the plane until they are no more than tiny dots in the huge blue, Pacific. The hustle-bustle is on again. Among the passengers there is a real end-of-term spirit. It's like a rich version of a trip to Minehead in a coach with the supporters club of the Scunthorpe Pigeon Fanciers Association, – I should think, never having fancied a pigeon myself. Still don't knock it until you've tried it. Penny, you're rambling. I dash about with the liquid refreshments, pouring extra large ones. Even our journalist friend is looking quite jolly again. And the terrible trio are subdued, which is how I like them. It promises to be a good flight.

Never believe a promise. We have a three-hour delay in LA owing to an industrial dispute among the ground crew. It is good to hear that other people have strikes as well as we British. It's hotter than hell in LA and a low smog hangs over the city. We sit in the plane for a while and then go to the terminal for a meal. By the time the ground staff have consented to refuel, tempers are getting a bit short.

'So this is what they call the glamour of flying,' says Kate.

'A life of high excitement, foreign travel, exotic cities and sitting on your backside.'

It's dark long before we touch down in Chicago again. We are doing a direct haul from there to London, ETA 8.00 am London time. The skipper announces that he will be endeavouring to make up an hour or two on the way back.

'Jolly good,' says Kate, 'give it a go Biggles old chap.'

It's been a long hard day and everyone falls fast asleep after dinner.

'Now Penelope Sutton, let's see what you can produce.'

'You just rest your little head there, and I'll be back, jockey shorts in hand in no time.'

As she dozes off, I go and find Ed.

'Sorry Penny, I forgot to put a spare pair in my overnight bag like we agreed. It will have to be the ones I have got on.'

'OK, well get them off, not here, in the loo I mean.'

'Tell you what, why don't I come down that lift with you?'

'It's not big enough, that's why.'

'Well I'll go first, you come down, I'll give you the jockey shorts, I come up, you come up, big smirk, you win the competition or whatever.'

'OK, see you in the galley in about five minutes.'

I go and busy myself there making a cup of coffee and tidying up. Ed arrives. I press the button for the lift and shove him in.

'Be sure to close the door when you get down there. It's a very tight fit.'

Down he goes. I give him a few moments to get his shorts off and his trousers back on and down I go. Unfortunately, he has forgotten to do the last part. As I come out of the lift into the little hold, he is standing there with his trousers hanging conveniently on a bottle of champagne poking out of the rack.

'I thought while we were down here we might as well do it right.'

He gives me a kiss. Even though my backside is against a shelf full of duty free cigarettes and my right boob is about to disappear into a consignment of vomit bags, I find the whole thing very exciting.

Ed manoeuvres himself round so that he is between me and the door. He shuts it and begins to undo the front of my blouse. With his free hand he is skilfully removing my tights. I realize there is no percentage in resisting, so I help him, and hang them and my panties on a bottle next to his trousers. He pulls my skirt up and begins to caress me with intent. My bra is pushed up around my neck and he tries to kiss my breasts. It looks as though he might put his neck out of joint but he succeeds.

Just as he is lifting me on to him, both of our backs leaning against the shelves, I hear a whirr and the lift goes up the shaft.

'Christ, who did that?'

'Don't worry, we'll get it back.

'I've got news for you, you can't get it back from here.'

'Oh well, let's make the best of it.'

There is very little room for manoeuvre, but somehow, by wrapping my legs around his thighs and my arms around his neck we manage to get it together. All other considerations apart, I don't think either of us is athletic enough to keep this up for more than a few minutes. We don't. It may not be the most comfortable lay I have ever had, but it certainly is the most gymnastic, and also one of the most exciting.

As we struggle to get our clothes back on – it's not easy in a space the size of a largish broom cupboard – I wonder what we can do about the lift. I don't want to shout, there's no form of communication with the upper deck and here we are, surrounded by cigarettes, booze and food.

'Not a bad fate really,' says Ed, as he uncorks a bottle of champagne. We drink about half of it. Ed gives me a deep kiss and begins to rummage under my skirt again.

'My goodness, we are frisky.'

'Come on.'

'I don't think I could go through all that undressing again and climbing up the shelf.' But I am weakening. Fortunately I am saved by the lift. Or rather by Kate. She comes down, opens the door and peeks in.

'What a lovely little love-nest. Give me the evidence and I'll send the lift down for you.'

I hand her Ed's pants. Very fetching tartan numbers, with his name in them on a little red tape.

CHAPTER FOURTEEN

London, dear old London. In point of fact Kate and I are
very depressed for a day or two when we get back. Jake is
nowhere to be found. His office says he is doing a recce,
whatever that may be.

Anyway, we hang about like the ghost of Christmas past
hoping for something to turn up. And it does. It always
seems to with us. It's an appearance at the airshow with
British-American, just being about and trying to look
interested. CJ it turns out has taken the decision himself
that we should be there as they launch their new planes and
their new routes. It's better than sitting in our bomb shelter
gathering bread mould I think. So does Kate.

'Better than a slap in the face with a wet bloater,' she
says with her superior choice of the right words.

'I wonder what happened to Dave and Jake?' I ask Kate.
'It's very mysterious that no-one has told us anything
about the rest of the filming.'

'I know. I can't imagine. Perhaps CJ will tell us. Penny,
you know I think old CJ has got his eye on us. It will be
a difficult number to get out of. I mean we owe everything
to him – our jobs, our prospects, our future.'

She lays it on with a trowel when she wants to, does our
Kate. Still, I see what she means. On the other hand, the
airline has spent a bomb on promoting us as their personality girls and as their ideal stewardesses, so they can't
really be prepared to chuck us out just cause the boss might
take a fancy to us which we don't return. Well, we can just
hope it doesn't come to that.

'Kate, we must just be a little careful. He thinks we are

easy game so he will try and get us into some sort of position to exploit it if he can. Keep alert. Be brave, be on your guard, be circumspect – and if all else fails, lie back and think of England.'

'Ta. I'll remember that.'

Our suspicions turn out to be well-founded. Old CJ has taken a private apartment in Knightsbridge, all Louis-the-something chairs and chandeliers, for the duration of the airshow, and he regards us as ornaments both on and off duty. We have to supervise the entertaining, as he puts it, which means running around with lots of boob and leg showing in those short, short skirts and loose tops for the amusement of his clients when they come back to the apartment or go to the company's stand in the exhibition hall. I begin to feel like a piece of public property. On the first day alone I get ten propositions and five phone numbers on scraps of paper.

'Perhaps we should go into the blackmail business. If some of these blokes' wives could hear the way they talk to us we could break up many a happy home in the stock-broker belt.'

'More like the garter belt.'

The number of unintentional brushes we have with wandering hands and other extremities is fantastic. I suppose when you are running around dressed the way we are, the public at large imagine you are some sort of convenience. They don't seem to realize that we are wearing these sexy blouses and little skirts because it's our job – God knows I wouldn't dress up like this to go to Sunday lunch with my mum. We escape the first day of the air show with nothing worse than a lot of pinches and propositions. CJ has an official engagement with the head of an Arab airline so we get away from his apartment quite early.

I can't wait to get some sensible clothes on, and I am doing just that, standing among the rubble drying myself after a cool bath, when the front door bell rings. I pull on a pair of panties, wrap myself in a towel and get to the door seconds ahead of Kate, who has only got a dressing gown on with her hair in rollers. It's Jake. I can't believe how ill he looks.

'Prison pallor,' he says when he sees me eyeing him anxiously. 'I'm a bloody criminal, we all look like this.' He kisses me and Kate both with real affection.

'Jake how are you, what's been going on? Oh I am glad to see you.'

'Get your glad rags on girls, I'll take you away from all this.'

'Where are we going?'

'Hell, I don't know, anywhere, I need cheering up. We look to be for the bloody high jump. You heard about our little run in with the fuzz?'

'I had heard something, yes. Is it serious?'

'Is it serious? Jesus, Dave could go down for two years and me for nine months, so it seems. Once those bastards get their hook into you it's not much fun. Come on, get dressed, don't stand there with your mouths open, you look like a pair of goldfish.'

We dress hurriedly. The Rolls is outside, which for some reason makes me feel that there just might still be some hope. As we swish towards Soho, I ask about Dave.

'Dave the druggist. He's in real bad trouble. They got all our bank records and it's obvious from that that I was just helping him in a spot of trouble. He hasn't paid any tax either for five years. He's falling apart, I mean they've got so much on him now that he could be in and out of court for years.'

'No wonder you two were behaving a bit strange in Paris.'

'Yeah, I'm sorry about that, but you can imagine at the time we had just heard what shit we were in, so our minds were elsewhere.'

We pull up outside the Trattoria Preciosa, to be engulfed by a tide of eager waiters and others.

'Bella signorina. Meester Cartnoy. Wonderful to see you. Have a drink on the house. I prepare the special Wormwood Scrubbs Cocktail.'

In Italian circles it seems to be an honour to have spent a few days in jail, sort of inevitable like getting married or having a serious illness, things from which you can recover if you adopt the right attitude.

'Christ, you would think I was Ronald Biggs. I have only been inside two nights on remand.'

'You're a hero.' Kate's eyes are shining as we try out Franco's special cocktail.

'I'm a bloody fool. And now I am going to spend the winter in the nick unless I can think of something.'

'Can't Dave tell them it was all his fault?'

'Yes, but the trouble is it wasn't all his fault. They were my film cans and it was my film company that transported the stuff. Franco, what have you put in this stuff?'

'Never mind, it's a special. We did one for Signor Kray and his brother once.'

'Thanks a lot. Jesus, these guys think I am a big time hood. Don't let on or we may not get any free champagne.'

Everything is free tonight. Jake is looking quite ill, from worry I suppose, but in fact he is more fun than ever, probably because it is all out in the open now.

'Look girls, I want you to do something to help us? OK?'

'Sure, if we can.'

'Explain the problem to that old shit CJ. He probably knows about it already, but suggest that there might be some scandal in it, you know filming for his airline and that, and see if he can do anything.'

'What can he do?'

'He can do quite a lot if he tries. I mean he knows the Home Secretary intimately. If they could just alter the charges slightly, I might get away with a suspended and a fine.'

'Well I'll see what I can do. He is pretty well trying to enrol us as his personal tarts even now with this air-show.'

'Yes, he's like that. But he understands a deal. We keep quiet about the airline, no stories out of school, he tries to fix something down at the Drug Squad.'

'Jake I will try. If I have to make a few small sacrifices for you, I will.'

'Good girl. I don't think we can save Dave from at least a short sentence, I mean he sold thousands, tens of thousands of pounds of dope, but at least I may be able to keep out. I don't see any advantage in going in the nick with the poor geezer, that's not going to help him and it's certainly not going to do anything for me.'

'I'll try too, Jake, for you and Dave.' Kate's eyes are moist with emotion.

We sound like people about to take the pledge. Still, Jake has such an appealing way about him, I don't mind him using us a little. He's done a lot for us in the past too. And if he gets sent down, we may not get to do the new commercials.

'What about the rest of the filming?'

'Well the ones we did were a huge success. We should get the rest of the business if it all goes OK. But I can't direct the bloody things from the Scrubbs, can I?'

'That's another good reason why CJ should try and keep you out of the news.'

'I'm in the news already, but until the evidence comes

out, the press are treating it as a minor drug offence. Not as interesting as a pop star or anybody important. Franco, let's have another bottle of your Barolo.' He's drinking like a man who wants to forget.

We have another bottle of that and another few bottles of this and that as well. By the time we get outside, Jake thinks he had better get a taxi and leaves his car in a car park. He is completely legless. Kate and I help him to bed, undress him, survey his thin, rather childish body regretfully and leave.

'He really is in a bad way, isn't he?'

'Yes, I suppose it's understandable.'

'You know what old CJ will want from us if we try to help, don't you Kate?'

'I am afraid I do.'

'Well, look, it's more my problem than yours Kate, if it comes to the crunch, leave him to me.'

'Penny, I have been in all sorts of situations with you. You have helped me out more than once. We'll go through with this together.'

'I think we must make more of an effort to be nice to CJ tomorrow, then in the evening when the going gets a bit rough round at Lowndes Square, lay it on the line.'

'Lay what on the line?'

'You know what I mean. Either he helps Jake and Dave, or we get out of the whole business.'

'Supposing he tells us to piss off?'

'He won't. For one he can't afford to – we are established all over the travel business as his personality girls, for two he's a randy old goat and for three there's the suggestion that if he doesn't help Jake the publicity is going to be terrible.'

'Jesus, Penny, I hope it works. We are getting into very deep waters here.'

Indeed we are. The morning begins with a few films and a trip round the mock-up of the interior of the plane. Kate and I point out the salient features of the new aircraft to a group of journalists and travel trade people, who seem more interested in our salient points. But in accordance with our resolution to do all we can to help Jake and Dave, I am extra nice to them all. I don't mind at all when they look down my cleavage as I demonstrate the new adjustable foot rest. In fact I have put on my sexiest, skimpiest three-quarter bra for the occasion. Kate similarly is wearing a bra which would not do justice to a twelve-year-old schoolgirl and her skirt seems to be endeavouring to creep up her back. She is a seasoned trooper at this sort of thing, but this performance is magnificent. By the time CJ appears, to deliver a little speech and preside over lunch, we have them eating out of our hands. It's amazing how you can use sex, or the suggestion of it, if you want to. Kate and I manage to convey to them the impression that we would run off at a moments notice with any of them for a bit of the other, if only we weren't busy just now.

CJ draws me aside as we go into lunch. His hand somehow finds its way on to my thigh as he talks.

'I believe you girls are doing a grand job today. Fantastic. It's just what we need. The personal, sexy touch in our promotion.'

'Anything for you, CJ,' I say, giving his hand a little squeeze.

He looks a bit startled.

'Yes, well, let's go and have lunch now. After you.'

I roll my hips in what I take to be a good imitation of Marilyn Monroe as I go in ahead of him.

Kate is practically devouring a potential customer as he talks. She is leaning forward so far that I suspect her boobs may join his melon on the plate in front of him in a moment. Actually she seems to be enjoying the game. I get going with a will, talking to everyone, telling them all about the plane and our flights and our new routes to South America, offering to help travel agents with their promotions, filling up glasses and generally being a little gem. CJ beams at us like a proud father. Well, more like a proud pimp really. He sidles up to me.

'Look, I am having a very important dinner this evening with the head of Anglo Associated Travel. Quite private, over at the flat, and I think it would help if you and Kate were there. I don't really want to talk business with the man, just get on good terms with him. You be there about nine, wear something sexy, not these uniforms, something elegant and we may go on to Annabel's if you are in the mood afterwards. OK?'

'We would love to. About nine, dress sexy. You're on.' I give him a deep meaningful look as I say it, and lick my top lip. Christ, I hope I am not overacting. He may be a bit of an old stoat, but he's not a fool. Must get this just right.

Dress sexy. Kate and I agonize over what to wear. Just as I am plumping for a knit dress with a silk shirt and a cleavage down to my waist, the phone rings. It's Jake.

'How are things? Sorry I crashed out last night but I had a bit too much to think about. Any progress with CJ?'

'Darling, don't worry, the first battalion, Dagenham Girl Pipers are going into battle even as we speak.'

'What do you mean?'

'Never mind. Here comes Sergeant Goodbody now. Here, have a word with Jake while I get my uniform on.'

God knows where Kate got the clothes. Looks like she borrowed them from the chorus line at the Folies. She is wearing a see-through blouse, and when Kate wears a see-through blouse there's a lot to see; a tiny black bra, long skirt slashed up the leg like a Chinese whore, her hair hanging loose over her shoulders, and a feather boa wrapped round her neck and strategically adjusted to prevent our being arrested right away for indecent exposure. It's a hell of an act to follow, but I don't think I am lagging too far behind in my clinging dress with only a flimsy silk shirt between me and total exposure. My panties are so small you can practically discount those.

'Do you think they will go for these suspenders?' asks Kate, pulling up her skirt.

'I should think so. What about this?' I point at my front.

'What do you want me to say? If you open it any more you'll have no need for a blouse at all.'

'Kate, a terrible thought has struck me.'

'Oh yes, what's that?'

'What we are doing is whoring.'

'Hell, it's what we do most of the time anyway; this time we are doing it for a noble purpose.'

'Just keep reminding me from time to time, won't you?'

'OK.'

And off we set for Lowndes Square. A manservant takes our wraps and shows us in to the flat.

'Ah here they are, my two little sweeties. Kate and Penny, I want you to meet Arnold Montgomery. Arnie, these are the personality girls, Kate Goodbody and Penny Sutton.'

Poor Arnold. His beady eyes seem transfixed by Kate's cleavage, which is truly stunning. He is not big, but he has a small, dynamic look about him, like a fox terrier or a scrum half at rugby. (I have an intimate knowledge of rugby, painfully acquired following a large rugby player for a whole season). His keen eyes dart from Kate's cleavage to my boobs, two thirds of which are peeping out. He looks as though he thinks he might have died and gone to heaven.

'Arnold, it is certainly a pleasure to meet you.'

'It's a pleasure to meet you too.'

'Now my dears have a drink' says CJ who is nattily attired in a blue velvet smoking jacket, so natty in fact that he looks like Sherlock Holmes about to sally forth from Baker Street to run his swordstick up someone's jumper. Actually, the only jumper he thinks he might be running it up is mine, and it's a prospect I don't relish, much. The only remedy is to take a few large drinks fast and go on from there. I am quite nervous.

'I think I'll have a vodka and tonic, not too much tonic, please CJ. You are looking handsome tonight, even more so than usual.'

CJ is tickled. 'Aren't they a lovely pair,' he says, 'they are doing wonders for our promotion you know. Just swept all before them in Hawaii, I want you to know. Still, we promised not to talk shop this evening didn't we Arnold? No, no tonight is for pleasure, eh what?'

'You're so right CJ.' I coo. 'Come Arnold, come and sit with me over here on the sofa.'

Arnold takes a flying leap. This little fellow looks as though he is made of rubber. I sit next to him, my knee brushing his trousers gently. He needs very little encouragement to tell me all about his business, and then about his roses, and before I know it I have had another large vodka and then a third. I begin to feel decidedly woozy, but if this is going to be my entry into the world of prostitution, I don't want to be too conscious.

Dinner is quite marvellous. We sit at a small, round table in the penthouse, overlooking most of Knightsbridge. Arnold's rubbery little hands find their way on to my thighs more than once as we eat. Every now and then I catch Kate looking a bit startled as though she has sat on a drawing pin or something, and wonder what old CJ is up to under the table.

Between the hors d'oeuvres and the main course, Arnold

tries to stick his hand up under my dress. I remove it with a smile, and pat his thigh.

'Now don't be impatient Arnold old thing.'

We drink copious amounts of wine and then brandies. Arnold and CJ light up two of the biggest cigars you can imagine.

'Now serve the coffee in the drawing room, Shirtcliffe, and you can retire.'

'Very good sir. The port and the brandy are on the sideboard. Goodnight sir, goodnight Madam.' Touch of the Upstairs, Downstairs.

Off he goes, as discreetly as a bookie on wheels. Now the action is going to begin, I surmise. I surmise correctly. CJ puts an old Sinatra track on his Hi-Fi and asks Kate to dance. She gets up unsteadily and shuffles round the floor with him.

'Come on Arnold, let's not be wallflowers.' Arnold leaps to his feet agilely enough, but can't stay standing too firmly. I don't feel so good myself. I see a ray of hope in this fact. Maybe he will be too drunk to perform if it comes to that, which it surely will at this rate. He presses me to him and I breathe in his ear a bit. His hands begin to wander over my boobs, which I must admit do look as though they are being put out on display, like apples in a street market.

'Now, now Arnold, let me have another drink first. Here you have one too.' It's an old trick, but a good one. He swallows a large port so fast I have hardly got the glass to my lips before he is whirling me around the carpet, bumping into the furniture from time to time in his excitement.

Kate is doing no better. CJ has unbuttoned the front of her see-through blouse and is endeavouring to unhook her bra. She is playfully trying to stop him. And all the time they are vaguely dancing to 'Strangers in the Night'. Actually I think it's a very apt title, which makes me laugh. I begin to giggle hysterically. I am completely pissed if the truth be told, which it must. But poor old Arnold is beyond even that. All the excitement seems to have gone to his head along with all the drink, and he can no longer stand. It reminds me of the ten little niggers. If we can only get rid of CJ we might come out of this intact. We let Arnold subside on to a sofa, and then I ply CJ with another brandy. But he is made of sterner stuff than that.

'Well, well, it looks like it's got to be just the three of us. Poor Arnold – nice chap you know, a Rotarian and a good family man. Come with me.'

The three of us stagger into the bedroom. I decide that before this gets going I had better make my point about Jake.

'CJ there is just one thing.'

He is already removing his trousers.

'What's that?'

'Well it's about Jake and David and the drugs charge.'

'Oh don't worry about that, I'll have a word in the morning with Hubert at the Home Office.

'Good.'

'Now how about a little bottom spanking eh? You've been naughty girls wearing these sexy clothes in school. Very naughty. Bend over. That's it, take your panties off. You deserve this you know, because you've been very naughty.'

Good God, if Jake could see us now, the two of us bottoms up on CJ's bed getting vigorously spanked by the Chairman of British-American Airways, he would award us a medal. And CJ is only wearing his socks.

CHAPTER FIFTEEN

In some small way, which I don't fully understand, the charges are altered which make the whole crime far less serious. Instead of trading in marijuana and suchlike noxious substances, they are charged with possession, and the lawyers are unanimous in thinking that it's just a fine and possibly a suspended sentence for Dave. People have had their bottoms spanked for less.

Actually our little number with CJ was fairly harmless really. Although the world would label him as kinky, he just likes to spank girls' bottoms. It's not my scene, but I certainly wouldn't condemn him for it. Still, Kate and I find it a little hard to sit down at the moment – before he subsided in a heap on the Burgundy Axminster carpet, old CJ managed to land some pretty nifty blows on my bare cheeks. To be honest Kate and I find the whole thing a bit of a giggle, but we aren't going to tell anyone about it, that's for sure.

'How did you get the old goat to do something about it?' asks a grateful Jake.

'Ask no questions, get told no lies. Now get us into that old banger of yours and take us out where the music is low, the food is divine and the cushions on the chairs are soft as swansdown.'

He can't understand our mirth. 'Hold on a moment, I have an old friend of yours coming round in a moment and he is suitably grateful.'

Almost on cue, Dave comes bounding in the door. 'I don't know how you did it, but thank you, thank you. Jesus, I don't think prison would have suited me, my complexion is too delicate for that cold air. Anyway I'm far too beautiful to go to prison, I would become a target for the older type of con's lust.'

'You would have liked that. He's very disappointed actually.'

'Go and screw yourself,' he says amiably. 'No girls I am so grateful to you and your intercessions with CJ who in turn nobbled some high-up in his club in St James's that I have brought a little present for you both.'

'Don't let him grab all the glory. I chose it.'

Dave gives us each a little parcel. We open them to find beautiful Cartier wrist watches. My, they are grateful. Today everyone likes us. C.J. has been ringing, continually, but we are trying hard to be out. I mean we feel once is enough as far as he is concerned.

'Sit down, Penny, for Chrissakes, you are making me nervous standing around.'

'No thank you, I would just as soon stand for the moment, thanks.'

'Well come on, we've got another surprise for you too. If you won't sit down, we might as well go.'

We jump into the Rolls and head for Mayfair, to a small theatre, all very plush with velvet curtains and huge armchairs. At Jake's command the curtains swing back and the screen lights up. My goodness, the boy is an artist. Out of all that confusion in the aircraft and in Paris he has made a beautiful sixty seconds of film. The music is strong and memorable, Kate and I look terrific, and the whole airline comes across as swinging, friendly and sexy.

'Jake you're a genius. Can we see it again?'

'See that look on Penny's face, that's when she saw the flasher at work.'

Far from being a flasher, the old priest looks the kindest, sweetest old gent in the world. I wish they had a shot of him chopping down the toilets with his axe. As I watch I feel as though I want to rush out and book a trip immediately.

'British-American, we'll take you the whole way,' says a sexy voice as the sun sets over Paris and Kate and me too. I feel like a star.

'They go on the air in a week and then you two girls will be seen in every household in Britain and maybe some abroad as well.'

Now I understand why they pay Jake so well. He really has made the thing very persuasive, and all in sixty seconds. And what they have done for Kate and me is something else. We look so relaxed, so pretty and yet sexy. Jake knew exactly the effect he was striving for and now I also understand why we had to do every take so many times.

'Well, bloody fantastic aren't they?' says Jake modestly.

'On Monday we are off to New York to film some more,' adds Dave.

'Always assuming they don't put us in the nick on Friday.'

Friday is the day they are to appear in Uxbridge magistrate's court. Then New York for a week's filming. I know New York quite well having flown there a lot in the past, but I still find it one of the most exciting places I've ever been to. Oh it all seems to be working out so well.

We leave the theatre and go out to one of those long, carefree lunches that I love so much. At least I love them until five o'clock in the afternoon which is usually about the time one begins to sober up. But today is different. We all go back to Jake's place in Covent Garden and drink some much needed black coffee before Jake and I retire to his bed for a slow and gentle, drowsy session of lovemaking. I fall peacefully asleep even before he is finished – into a deep, contented sleep. For me this is a bad sign; it usually means I am falling in love. Some people can't concentrate, some people eat too much, others too little, some people read poetry, others go for long, solitary walks. But I sleep like a baby.

'You're in love again, Penelope,' says Kate firmly.

'How do you know?'

'My God, since that day we met at the training centre so long ago I've observed you at close quarters with heaven only knows how many men. I know. Just accept the fact that you are in love.'

'OK, if you say so. What about you?'

'Well after you two randy beasts slunk off to bed yesterday, Dave and I didn't want to feel left out of things, so we sort of flopped into the other bed.'

'OK?'

'Terrific. The only thing is I think he felt he was being dutiful, you know because of what we had done for them. Anyway we went out to the theatre later, leaving you two lying there as though you had been pole-axed.'

'I know, we didn't wake up until midnight.'

'All the old signs. Look at the bloom on your cheeks. You look like a bloody milkmaid.'

'Well I feel quite relaxed, and everything is going so well. Aren't you looking forward to New York?'

'I am indeed. The only trouble is, I don't think we will be going.'

'Why not?'

'I don't know, I just have a feeling.'

'Don't be so pessimistic. What can go wrong?'

'Well, when I am on the plane on Monday morning I'll believe it.'

'Goodness me, you are a downer. I bet you they get off lightly on Friday, then off we go.'

They do get off lightly on Friday. It is almost shameful how quickly and simply the whole thing is handled. To the outsider it looks as though everyone is playing a part in a play that has been very well-rehearsed. The fines are stiff, Dave gets a suspended sentence of three months and they are out of the court in twenty minutes.

'Penny, I really want to thank you for your efforts. You know I mean this, don't you?'

'Yes, Jake, I think you do.'

'So we'll see you on Monday at Heathrow. Don't be late, the car will pick you up at your place at six-thirty.'

'Well where are you going until Monday?'

'I've still got a lot to do. I won't be in town. Bye now.'

He hops into his Rolls and leaves us standing on the corner outside our flat.

'So much for romance,' says Kate. 'How do you pick them, Penny?'

'I don't know. We save the bastards from a career of breaking rocks, they give us a little present like a pair of children who have been good, and then, woosh, you can't see them for dust.'

'Don't worry, something will turn up, as Mr Pickwick said.'

'It wasn't Mr Pickwick . . . quick, look, it's Ed.'

He is obviously used to being waved at by strange girls, is Ed, because he smiles at us vaguely, and tries to hurry past.

'Got something to hide, have you?' I say grabbing his arm.

'Penny, what a lovely surprise, you know for a moment I thought you were fans. Still, my fan died last year, so it was optimistic of me. How are you girls? You look wonderful. What you up to? Nothing? My God what's wrong with the young men of London these days? How about spending the week-end with me down at my place in the country? Nothing special, just a little riding and a few laughs and jokes. OK? Great, I'll meet you at the Cavendish at six and we'll go down together. No don't worry, I'll ring the house-keeper and tell her to make up some beds. Smashing, must go now, I'm being interviewed by Capital Radio. What do I think of the economic recession in the theatre, a light-hearted viewpoint? That's me. See you.'

How old Ed cheers us up. He seems to be so full of life that it spills over and touches everybody else.

'What have we agreed to?'

'I don't know, but it will be better than hanging around in London, terrified to answer the phone in case it's old CJ inviting us to come round for a little flogging with some more of his business contacts.'

'Too true. I doubt if my bottom is up to horseriding even now.'

'Rub a little whisky on it. I read somewhere that that does wonders for it.'

'Kate you're a pal. Let's go and pack.'

Ed's place, as he calls it, seems to be buried in the heart of a great big private forest, somewhere near Ascot. The woods are full of huge houses, each set in five or six acres; we make our way up a positive warren of private roads until we come to Ed's house. It is mock Tudor, but so enormous it was obviously never intended to house anyone less than a millionaire. Anyway, who ever heard of an Elizabethan house with an indoor swimming pool? It backs on to the golf course, clearly something a bit sacred around here. The course looks pretty enough, I must say, though golf is something which leaves me stone cold.

'Ed this is fantastic.'

'Not bad for a lad who was booed off the stage in the Astoria, New Cross in his youth, is it?'

'No I'll say it isn't. What's that over there?'

'That my dear, is the centre of the Wentworth and District Wife Swapping Society. It's a cultural improvement I have made to the neighbourhood. Come inside and I'll show you what goes on.'

Inside is a giant sauna, swimming pool and gym, built in the old stables of the house.

'Yes, we have some pretty merry goings on around here of a week-end I can tell you.'

'And this is a week-end,' remarks Kate intelligently.

'You had better believe it is,' says Ed, 'why do you think I invited you? For the golf?'

You can't keep a straight face with him about, which is lucky because we are feeling a bit glum at our treatment from Jake and Dave. I mean deep down I am a one-man girl – it's just that there are so many distractions along the way.

'So who is for a swim?'

We all plunge naked into the pool which is deliciously warm. Afterwards Ed gives us Japanese robes to wear round the house, which are, so he says, all he ever wears at home.

'Tomorrow I am playing golf most of the day, but I'll fix some riding for you and then a few people are coming over for dinner. Both of you ride? I can't. My dad used to have a horse when I was a kid, used to pull a rag and bones cart. Finally the old horse died trying to take me mum's furniture up to the pawnbrokers. The whole lot slipped down a hill, dead horse, furniture, cart, dad, me mum and all and ended up in a funeral parlour, just as they were laying out a dead jellied eel salesman. Ruined the arrangements completely, said the undertaker. Not to mention me mum's furniture.

'I'll never forget that, ruined the arrangements the man kept saying as I appeared with the coppers. The horse was lying, crafty old thing, with his head in a pile of wreaths, looked like he had fetched up in the last great grazing ground in the sky, lucky devil. The jellied eel salesman was covered in embalming fluid, and his trousers were still round his ankles, which is as far as they had got after anointing his body. Terrible bloody commotion. Put me right off horses as a means of transport, I can tell you. At least a Jag can't have a heart attack.'

'What about tonight?'

'Well, tonight I thought we might see some movies. I have a cinema down in the basement. We'll get a few of my chums over from the surrounding hovels and watch movies, play games and drink a bit. Now how about some dinner for you lovelies. Come on.'

His housekeeper obviously worships him. He gives her a kiss and we sit down to eat, still in our robes.

'What you got for us today, Florrie?'

'Your favourite.'

'What's my favourite then?'

'You know what you like.'

'What?'

'Tripe and onions.'

'Terrific.'

Kate and I go a bit green at the mention of tripe, but you don't turn down the food in someone else's house. I try not to think what part of the animal it is as I ease a bit into my mouth. To my amazement I find it delicious. Kate looks apprehensive too, but she also enjoys it, it turns out.

'Marvellous isn't it?'

'To be honest Ed, I've always steered well clear of it. But it's great.'

'Puts lead in your pencil.'

'I haven't got a pencil.'

'The operation is painless. I'll give you the address of my brother the surgeon. Have you heard the story of the

President Nixon and the arse-hole transplant . . . no? the arsehole rejected Nixon.'

He laughs so much that I suspect he might fall off his chair. After dinner he gets on the telephone and in no time the house is full of the most incredible assortment of people.

'I've invited a few of the neighbours around. Here, General, this is Penny and this is Kate.'

Can he really be a general? He can. He lives nearby in an equally large house, though in his case, he tells us, he inherited it. I think he fancies Kate, which is OK by me so I wander off with Ed and a few others leaving them discussing polo. In his private cinema we sit down, drinks in hand to see Deep Throat.

'I thought it was banned in this country,' I say innocently.

'My darling, if we were not allowed to see or do all the things that some people disapprove of, life would be a much poorer experience.' The man speaking, I find out later is a leading barrister. Deep Throat seems to be remarkable only as a circus trick. As Dr Johnson said, it is not done well but you are surprised to find it done at all – and he wasn't talking about sword-swallowing, either. After the first ten minutes I am bored by watching male members disappearing into unlikely places – the men seem to find it fascinating however, and some of the women are beginning to twitch a bit.

'Get's them in the mood,' says Ed with a chuckle, 'come on let's go and see how the others are getting on.'

In the sauna, some of the others are getting on all too well.

'That's what I like to see. Liven up old England, that's my motto. I am a one-man filth brigade.'

In fact, nothing could be further from the truth. Even though Ed has no morals in the conventional sense, he is the kindest, jolliest soul I have ever met. He is so concerned that everyone should have a good time.

'Look at this, two pop stars, a general, a barrister, one stockbroker, one actor, assorted girls, a footballer, lots of housewives and they're having a great time. People should give up sitting at home watching telly and get out and meet each other. I mean suddenly you're dead and what are you left with? Not a lot. David Coleman, Reginald Bosanquet and Eddie Waring aren't coming to your funeral, are they? When I go, the church is going to be so crowded they'll be selling tickets at the door. I'll pop out of the coffin for a quick one before they close the lid.'

In a curious way, his philosophy and mine are much the same. I think you should never pass up an opportunity when it comes your way. It's got me in a lot of trouble, but I've also had a good time as a result. And there's plenty of opportunity here. So to hell with Jake and his friends, and to hell with pining away.

Kate seems to be adopting the same attitude; she and the general are romping about in the sauna with the others, his silvery moustache and distinguished grey hair still very neat despite the temperature. I take off my robe and lie down on my front.

'Anyone for a birching?'

It's the barrister. He obviously regrets the day they banned flogging and capital punishment. In his hands he holds a bundle of twigs, like an old fashioned egg-whisk. I should introduce him to CJ.

'Birching? Larching?'

'No thanks, not today, I ran into a larcher the other day and haven't fully recovered.'

'Rub whisky on it, does wonders for it.'

'I see you read the same books as I do.'

'Larching, birching?' He plies his wares elsewhere. One not-so-young woman accepts and he flicks her all over with the bundle of twigs, which you can see even from where I am lying is doing wonder for his circulation. They exchange roles after a while. Soon they leave the sauna altogether for more private parts, no pun intended. Quite good that really, leave for more private parts.

There's something odd about a sauna, it leaves you feeling healthy but slightly sexless. I find that anyway. I must admit that it seems to be turning some of the others on, but as the heat gets higher, I begin to wilt completely. Stage two of the sauna is having a plunge in the special icy plunge. That really takes the breath away. Ed puts it differently.

'Freeze the balls off a brass monkey,' he shouts, as he jumps in after me.

'Last one to the other end is a monkey's nuts.'

This is a bit unfair, because I know from Hawaii that he can't swim. But he grabs me by the arm and embraces me:

'We can't go on meeting like this, Penelope, people are beginning to mutter.' My teeth are beginning to mutter, I can tell you. He pretends not to notice, and kisses me. My nipples are actually blue by the time he lets me get out.

'Who is the monkey's nuts now?'

'I doubt if you've got any by now; you're a eunuch.'

I race back to the sauna. In a corner two people are entwined like teenagers in the back seat of a mini. It's Kate and the general, I am afraid to say. I only hope he doesn't have a heart attack – it's at least a hundred and ten degrees in here and even if he is as fit as a sepoy on extra rations, this might be chancing his arm a bit.

So the evening progresses in jolly fashion. To tell the exact truth it degenerates a bit. I am not really in the mood for energetic entertainment of the sort most of the men seem to have in mind. It's curious how the fact that I am an air stewardess excites men. Most of the girls I know who fly report the same thing. I think there is a rumour about that stewardesses are all ravers. I wonder if we are any different from your normal, red-blooded young girl. The difference is that we are always on display for men and mostly we are looking after men, so they draw the wrong conclusions. Anyway, it's quite difficult in the normal course of events to get to know the passengers on a flight – everyone is in such a hurry when they get to the other end. Still, as I was saying, men do have this image of stewardesses, shared I believe with nurses and barmaids, that we are great little goers. I have to reject all sorts of offers, including a rather interesting one to come for a walk around the golf course from a bloke whose wife has just disappeared into the sauna with a pop musician. I've never been in a bunker.

I see a face I know from somewhere. It's a well-known international footballer, whose club is struggling to avoid relegation. He isn't going to be in any state to help them tomorrow, that's for sure. Not if he gets inside that robe with the tarty redhead he's with, which seems more than likely. Still, as Ed points out, if you had to play Manchester United tomorrow, you would be trying to forget.

'Hello, Kate, enjoy your military manoeuvres?'

'Quite a lot actually, Penny, if you must know. Come with me, I need a drink and a sit down.'

'What do you think? Looks like it could be some week-end, this?'

'You're not kidding. I knew we would never get to New York – we'll be too exhausted.'

'Where's the general?'

'I had to abandon him. His heart was beginning to flutter.'

CHAPTER SIXTEEN

Our week-end passes in a haze of alcohol and parties. Actually Kate and I lay off the sauce a bit after that first night because we want to look our best for New York, but the Wentworth and District Wife Swapping Club certainly get into their stride.

'No swinger like a middle-aged swinger,' remarks Kate sagely.

'You should know dear. I should think the general and his chums will erect a monument to you when they recover.'

Ed is particularly happy on the Sunday because he has played in a pro-am tournament with Gary Player or someone like that and they have won the tournament. It amazes me how passionate he is about golf, but chacun a son goat, I always say when in France or whatever turns you on, as the Americans say. If it's walking round a nice field hitting a little white ball, then that's your business. For myself I can think of many more amusing and interesting ways of passing the time.

Kate and I go riding, something which we do very occasionally and very badly at that. The stables look so smart that if one of the horses does a pile you feel you should start sweeping it up instantly. My horse is so shiny I can almost see my face in him. His face is large, aristocratic and slightly crafty. He is so big I think a crane would be more appropriate than the leg-up the lad is offering me. Still, after a little initial confusion during which the horse wears the equine equivalent of one of those ''ullo, got a right one 'ere', looks, I manage to get aboard.

Kate is not so fortunate, although the lad is, because she is wearing such tight jeans she can hardly bend her legs, let alone get up on the gee-gee. He pushes, she pants, and eventually there is a rending sound as her over-strained Levis give way all along the bottom seam, exposing a delightfully summery pair of yellow panties. For a moment the lad looks as though he might offer to take the saddle's place, but in the end he composes himself enough just to wear a smirk. Talk about a smirk, her horse is killing himself laughing. Still it's such a well-bred establishment, nobody says anything nasty although the lad's horse breaks wind rather emphatically as we set off into the woods.

Soon we get our confidence because the horses are so well-behaved, rather like elderly assistants at Fortnum and Mason, very trustworthy and decorous. Mine, when it understands what I want, which is difficult at first for the poor beast, does it without a murmur. Off we trot over the beautiful bridle paths in the forest. I have time to take stock of the countryside and our companion.

'What's your name?'

'Wilbur, madam.'

'How old are you, Wilbur?'

'I am sixteen, madam.'

'For Chrissake stop calling her madam, that's her trade not her name.' Witty old Kate.

'You're a very good-looking boy, Wilbur. Are you a professional horseman?'

Poor lad, he doesn't know what to make of his barrage from the two of us. But he has been nicely brought up, that's clear and is used to a better class of client than us. But Ed's name carries a bit of weight around here.

'I am training to be a show-jumper, and I teach and take rides as well.'

'I see. Have you done any jumping yet?'

Kate bursts our laughing, but the lad does not get the joke. Or if he does, he is subtler than he looks. He sits there on this great big grey horse, so straight you would think he had a poker in his hacking jacket. Flat cap, immaculate breeches, fawn sweater, knitted tie, and black boots. He ignores our coarse laughter and says, 'Yes, I won the junior competition in the South of England show this year. Now I am actually a senior.'

'Good heavens South of England jumping competition. You should enter Kate, you're a natural.'

'Do you jump?' He looks at Kate a bit sceptically.

'Goes like a Mexican jumping bean on heat.'

'Penny, shut up, you'll give the boy ideas.'

'How about trying a little canter now?'

'OK Cowboy, take it away.'

He canters off into the distance. Our horses follow sedately, like armchairs on legs. It's remarkably comfortable, except that I am not wearing a bra and it's a little bouncy.

'It makes me randy, all this jiggering up and down,' says Kate.

'For God's sake, Kate. If he hears he's going to get a warped idea of what goes on in the world. You and your bloody yellow panties, I bet he can hardly stay in the saddle now.'

'Do him good, give him a bit of a thrill.'

In his nice way he does a bit of showing off, making his horse leap over logs and even a gate for our benefit. I am glad to say our horses take not a blind bit of notice and just keep going in a sensible straight line. I could really enjoy riding with a bit of practice. Still, you would need to like gardening as well to make use of the manure.

'Wilbur, stop now, we're tired. Let's walk a bit.'

'Have you had enough?' he asks in a slightly superior sort of way.

'Well the General is getting on a bit, you know, so I suppose I could use a bit more.'

I try to give Kate a kick, but there is mischief in the air. I succeed in kicking her horse instead, who immediately breaks into a trot, Kate is quite unprepared and loses her stirrups. She is bouncing round like a sack of potatoes and is obviously going to land on her backside, but Wilbur is equal to the occasion. He grabs her round the shoulders, steadies her, gathers up her reins for her and stops the horse.

'Wilbur, you're my hero.' She gives him a big, wet kiss on the mouth. Poor Wilbur, he is blushing furiously. I think.

'And as for you, Penny, you could have killed me.'

'Sorry, I meant to kick you, not that nice horsey. Sorry horse. What's his name, Wilbur?'

'He is called Winston.'

'Does he smoke cigars?'

'What? No horses don't smoke. He eats oats, and bran and nuts and . . .'

'Oh never mind.'

'Wilbur, do you mind if I take my top off, it is so hot and I do want to get a bit of a tan? You don't mind, do you?'

'Well we are entering a Royal Forest now, do you think it wouldn't be a bit disrespectful?'

'To whom?'

'To the Royal Family.'

Can this boy be serious? I have a horrid suspicion he is taking the piss, but you can't be sure with this tight-lipped sort. Kate obviously thinks the Royal Family would approve of her 36C black bra. Wilbur tries not to look, but as I point out there's not a lot else to see. Seen one tree you've seen 'em all. And Kate is somewhat unique in that department, too.

'Why don't you get your shirt off, Penny.'

'I will when we stop somewhere for our picnic, but I don't think even I want to be the first topless horsewoman in a Royal Park.

'Lots of monarchists round here today. The sun is lovely. Where are we going to stop, Wilbur?'

'We'll stop by the lake, which is about another mile. I've brought some sandwiches and a thermos.' He pats a leather pouch attached to his saddle. In fact the scenery is fantastic. How the other half live. This is only twenty miles or so from London, and apart from the planes roaring overhead to and from Heathrow, you would imagine you were in the wilds of Scotland or somewhere even more remote.

The little lake Wilbur is talking about proves to be clear and greenish, very inviting on this hot afternoon.

'Can we swim?'

'But you haven't got any bathing suits,' says crafty Wilbur. He has obviously realized that you just need to tell Kate something is impossible to get her going.

'Who needs a bloody bathing suit? Take the horses over there and don't look while we go in.'

We both strip off and go in. The water is cold as ice at first, but after a moment it's wonderful.

'Come on in, Wilbur the water is lovely.'

He ties the horse to a tree, strips off out of sight, and appears, hands modestly covering himself. At the last moment he runs and dives in.

'Big boy too.'

'Kate you are really becoming a bit too crude. Not that big, not from where I was.'

We begin to splash each other with water and swim about in the shallows. Wilbur can't believe he's not in a dream. Kate keeps popping enough of herself out of the water to entice him. I come up behind him as he swims and tickle him. He tickles me back. This could turn into something good. Kate grabs him from behind and her hands may well be where they didn't ought to be. Who can tell? Wilbur looks as though he'll drown of ecstasy.

'This is your present for saving me from a terrible fate, Wilbur.'

I thrust my boobs into his chest too, never one to be left out of the act. But poor Wilbur, his baptism at our hands is never allowed to continue. Suddenly we hear the thunder of horses hooves and there they go our three beauties, galloping round the lake in the direction of home. In his excitement at the prospect of joining us in the water, Wilbur has not tied up the horses too securely, I think I can say with some certainty, because even now they are vanishing from view back down the track into the woods.

'My clothes, my clothes. They are in the pouch on the saddle. Quick, what are we going to do?'

'Lie back and forget about the horsey world, Wilbur.'

'Poor Wilbur, will you be in trouble when the horses come roaring back with your clothes?'

'Will I be in trouble? Fucking hell, I'll be up shit creek.' Wilbur has lost his cool completely, again. He runs like a dervish up the bank, and I see him hastily putting on Kate's jeans with the split back and my shirt.

'You can borrow my bra, too if you like, Wilbur,' shouts Kate at his running figure.

After we have nearly drowned with mirth, I begin to see that all may not be plain sailing. Here we are, the afternoon is drawing on, and we have one bra, one pair of jeans and one shirt between us. Our guide and instructor is nowhere to be seen, and judging by the speed the horses were moving relative to his own speed, it will take him some while to catch up with them. Probably get to the stables about the time they finish their tea. And anyway, we don't really know the way back. These forests begin to look as impenetrable as the Amazon Basin now that Wilbur has gone.

'Tell you what, let's take turns wearing the bra, it's getting a bit chilly.'

'Shall we try and walk back to the camp?'

'Penny, I told you to stop watching that damn Survival programme on the television. We are not in Afghanistan or Saudi Arabia or Borneo, we are in an English forest, not far from Windsor, home of our Queen and her lovely family. Camp, my backside.'

'It's your blooming backside that got us into this mess.'

'He will be back, I have great faith in the lad.'

'He's probably gone back to the stables, complaining that he was dragged off his horse, raped and abandoned in the wilderness by two demented women.'

'You had a hand in it, I saw. More correctly on it. Disgusting. Corrupting young innocents.'

At that moment, the young innocent comes riding over the greensward, leading two horses. He looks quite fetching in my cerise blouse, I must say. He is in a very good mood.

'Knew where to look for them. Greedy devils, they were munching bluebells by the first gate. Took a bit of catching, but here we are. Now if you would hold them, I'll get dressed, then you can. We better get a move on going back, or I'll be in real trouble I can tell you.

We're like the Pony Express on the way back. No time to admire Kate's buttercup-coloured bum for Wilbur – he's determined to get back before they send out the search parties. It's quite exciting, really, though my legs, back, arms and bottom are aching by the time we near the stables. Wilbur slows to a walk, puts on his most relaxed expression, straightens his tie and his back, and we clop in a dignified fashion into the yard.

'Everything go hunky-dory Wilbur?' asks the boss.

'Yes thank you, Major, pretty routine really.'

I give Kate a funny look.

'Cocky little sod,' she mutters to me under her breath.

'Thank you Major,' I say, 'your boy Wilbur took us on a most interesting ride.'

'Little worried about Wilbur,' he says, 'getting a bit of a reputation as a lady-killer, you know the kind of thing, randy little bugger; nothing of that sort, I hope?'

'No need to worry Major Featherstone, he was propriety itself.'

Ed's chauffeur is waiting for us.

'Goodbye Wilbur, if you have trouble with show-jumping, you could always take up the other sort.'

He gives us a big wink. So he is not so dumb after all; he'll go far that lad. Back at Ed's another party is in progress.

'Hello General, how's your jumping these days?'

We slip off and have a long hot bath to get the aches out of our bones I feel as though I have been kicked by a horse not been for a ride on one. That and the lingering memory of CJ's favourite pastime, playing the kettledrum on my backside, combine to make me walk something like a duck.

'You're walking like a duck,' says Kate.

'You're walking like Monsieur Hulot, so belt up.'

'Who is Monsieur Hulot? Did we meet him in St Tropez, or was it at that bistro in South Kensington that serves the frogs legs in garlic.'

'Kate relax. Your brain obviously took a battering on that saddle. Have a drink.'

'What are you going to wear?'

'It doesn't matter much around here. You always end up

the same way however you try. Still, I think I will wear the St Laurent trouser suit, the one that fell off the lorry.'

'It looks it to. Looks like it was run over by a few lorries following on behind.'

She's just jealous. It is my sexiest outfit, black silk pyjamas, really. Kate once tried it on and couldn't get her boobs into it and has had a down on Yves ever since. Jake likes it which is why I like it, deep down. Wonder what Jake's up to? I feel a rising of resentment against him and Dave, abandoning us again with no excuse this time. Still, we shall see tomorrow. At least a week in New York with them may settle things one way or the other. Damn him.

Ed doesn't let us brood too long. You would think he would get tired of people because apart from the few hours he was playing golf yesterday, the place has been packed with all sorts. It's open house on a grand scale. No wonder he has to work so hard – it's a question of feeding the multitude. Tonight the multitude are mostly golfers and their ladies, though some of the regulars – like the general – are here. He seems to live in Ed's house.

'More fun over here really. Over at my place you can't escape the pictures of my ancestors. All bloody military men. All staring down severely on you. Everyone a bloody idiot. One of them escaped injury at the charge of the Light Brigade only because he was too drunk to get on his horse. No, I like it over here and I particularly like you. Eh, what, how about a little sauna?'

Kate and he go skipping off into the garden. I get picked up by an assistant golf professional, who seems less interested in golf than in getting inside my trouser suit with me. He is called Nigel, which is extraordinary for a golfer I would have thought, but he's not bad really. Still I am in no mood to tangle with anyone new this evening. Apart from anything else, my bottom is too sore from all that riding. We do have a few dances together and Nigel tells me about the lady golfers he coaches who keep hitting their balls into the rough so they can get hold of his. So he says. He thinks he's a bit of a joker, and more than a bit of a lover.

Finally I get rid of him. Ed saves me.

'Having a good time?'

'Not bad, though I could have done with seeing more of you.'

'Sorry. You know how it is being the host. Anyway, I always live as though today may be my last. Got to keep moving. Come, let's go and see how they're doing down at the sauna.'

'Ed I think Kate and I had better be getting home, we've got to be up at cockcrow tomorrow for New York.'

'If you can find Kate, I'll have my chauffeur standing by. Last seen with the general playing horsey-horsey in the sauna.'

'Come on Kate, get your clothes on, we must go. Are you sure he's not dead?'

'Not him. He's just having a nap. A bit shagged out after a long sauna. Learned the habit in India, don't you know, quick naps to get up the strength in the middle of a campaign. Works wonders on the fuzzies.'

Is that an ambiguous remark, or do I just have a dirty mind? I don't ask.

CHAPTER SEVENTEEN

'Well here we are.'

'Don't speak too soon, we're not airborne yet.'

'Well, come on, short of a hijacking or the plane not being there, we're surely going to be aboard and away in under an hour.'

We are speeding out to the airport in a chauffeur-driven car sent by Jake. Yet Kate still doesn't believe all is going well.

At the check-in desk we find Jake and Dave with their habitual mountain of overweight. No sign of Mike yet.

'Hi girls, have a nice week-end?'

'Terrific, thanks.'

'Why are you both walking so funny?'

'What's funny about the way I'm walking?'

'Well, you're sort of waddling.'

'You're walking like Monsieur Hulot, Kate.'

'It's a long story,' I say, 'and this is neither the time nor the place.'

It takes ages to get aboard. Airlines are naturally a bit suspicious of piles of equipment, most of which looks like bazookas or rockets or bombs, as camera equipment tends to when in its metal boxes. Jake and Dave have to explain in every last detail to the security men. Mike turns up, late as ever, to help at the last moment.

'Well, well, if it isn't the pocket-sized Romeo. How are you, Mike?'

'Not bad, not bad. How about you two? You're walking a bit funny but otherwise you look fine.'

'Jesus, not another one. You look a bit odd yourself.'

'Yes, well my wife took a golf club to me the other night when I got in a wee bit late and she sort of altered the shape of my nose.'

'Very becoming. I thought you had had a nose job for a moment.'

'No, wouldn't want to gild the lily. Far too lovely already.'

'If you like midgets.'

'Tssk, tssk. We are in a good mood.'

Eventually we get aboard.

'Well, Kate, are we on board or are we not?'

'We are on board, I'll grant you that.'

'But?'

'But I don't think things are going to go OK.'

You can't reason with a mad person, it's best just to humour them and hope it passes away. So I sit with Jake and Dave and leave Kate brooding to herself on the other side of the aisle. We do have something to worry about, actually, and that is that our own friendly cabin crew turns out to be none other than the awful Kerry, of Hawaiian fame.

'Hello dear, bring us a drinky there's a good thing.'

'Oh no, not you again. I thought you had got out of my life for good.'

'My old friend, Stewardess Goodbody is here too, over there – I am sure she will be pleased to see you.'

'Yes, well, got a bit of work to do. Bye for now.'

We take off with that great surge of power. I look over at Kate. She shrugs as though she still can't believe it.

'Sorry we had to scarper on Friday,' says Jake disarmingly, 'but there's a lot of preparation for a trip like this, as you know.'

I melt shamefully. He is in such a good mood, lighting mammoth cigars, ordering drinks, being warm and attentive, that I am just glad to be with him again, and almost regret all the hard thoughts I have had about him over the last few days. As Kate says, I do know how to pick them. They are always rich, charming, handsome and bastards. Still, I don't think I am quite ready for the settled, suburban type yet. When that day dawns I will recognize it, give up flying, give up men, give up travelling and settle down somewhere with a Cortina and a few children. What a horrible prospect. For the moment I banish all such thoughts, particularly as Jake is applying his lovely lips to my left ear.

'I've missed you. I really have. These last few weeks have been worrying for us. You haven't seen me at my best. Now you will.'

'Is that a promise?'

'Sure. After we have finished filming, I'll take you round the States. There are some lovely places I know and a lot of mates of mine are scattered about. We'll go and see them. A good long holiday. Just the two of us.'

'Oh Jake, that would be terrific. With you I would go on holiday to Albania, if you wanted.'

He kisses me. I feel so happy, I don't even care when Kerry spills the champagne down my front. Poor girl is obviously envious of such contentment.

New York is like a giant factory. As a taxi driver once told me, it makes London look like a cemetery with the lights on. We sweep over Manhattan, with the Empire State Building so close you feel you could reach out and touch it, and then across to the airport.

'Exciting, isn't it? Still you've been here even more often than I have. But it is so big, so pulsating, the ultimate city.'

Blasé Dave is asleep, but I agree with Jake completely. Nonetheless, there is nowhere but London that I would really like to live, not for now anyway. New York is one of those places that is wonderfully exciting to visit.

'Kate, hello, Kate, we're here. Now do you believe it?'

'No.'

Nobody likes to make predictions that come out wrong, least of all our Kate. Trouble is, she's not wrong.

As we pass through customs two men in shiny mohair suits come up to us.

'Mr von Cartnoy? Mr Stanstead?'

'Yes.'

'Federal agents, come this way please.'

'Show me your identification.'

'Here you are sir.'

They lead Jake and Dave away and we are left standing there with Mike and a huge pile of luggage. Of course Mike has not a clue what to do, so I take charge.

'Christ, it was the FBI, just like in the movies,' says Mike.

'Now look, we must get hold of British-American's manager here at the airport and tell him quick,' say I. My training is coming in useful.

'I told you so, I told you,' says Kate.

'Wonderful. You get this month's special soothsaying award, now go and find the manager's office and bring him here fast. I'll get the rest of the stuff checked through.'

The manager is horrified. 'The scandal, I mean you are here under our auspices, I must get on to London immediately.'

'Why don't you find out what they're being done for, then get on to London? Maybe that would be a better way of going about it. Come on, let's find them.'

We can't. They have been taken to an FBI office somewhere. In the end the three of us check into our hotel and wait for news, I ring CJ in London, but he has obviously got a lawyer with him because he just tells me everything is in hand. Whatever that may mean. And also he tells us firmly not to talk to anyone.

'Can't you speak to the Home Secretary?'

'The Home Secretary ceased having jurisdiction in America in 1776. Now goodbye.'

'Goodbye to you.'

All that evening we sit miserably round the hotel lobby waiting for a call. It does not come. We go to bed with a bottle of bourbon, wondering what to do. Mike is no help at all – he just begins to panic, quite sure he is going to be arrested as an accessory for some ghastly crime.

In the morning the local boss of the airline sends for us. We go round to his office in Park Avenue.

'Girls, through no fault of your own, London has decided that you had better be kept right out of all this. Your friends Mr Stanstead and Mr von Cartnoy have been arrested for drug smuggling. Apparently Scotland Yard passed some information on to our local people about alleged offences. And in this country smuggling drugs across a Federal border is a matter for the FBI.'

'But they were fined in England.'

'Not for the smuggling they did into this country, I believe. And here it's a very, very serious offence.'

'What are we going to do? Where are they?'

'They are being held in a Federal prison on Staten Island until such time as bond can be posted. The authorities are going to ask for a hundred thousand dollars.'

'Where can they raise that sort of money?'

'Precisely. They can't.'

'Why don't you help?'

'As CJ has pointed out to me in a long telex, they are not our employees, but employees of our advertising agent,

Nutley Bratwurst and Cutlet. We are not responsible for them. In fact we disassociate ourselves completely from their activities.'

'What about us? We are your employees.'

'Precisely. CJ has requested that you fly back to London immediately. I have made all the arrangements. He feels, and I agree, that with our latest advertising push in America, the less you are associated with this matter the better. You are after all our Personality Girls.'

'Bollocks to your Personality Girls. We want to see Jake and Dave.'

'That will be impossible. No visitors until they are bailed, and there is no hope of their being bailed, so my attorney tells me, before Friday, even if they can raise the cash.'

'Terrific. So we get shipped off out of the way, and they spend their time languishing in prison because you won't bail them.'

'No, we won't and we have advised our advertising agency not to help either. In fact I believe the agency is preparing to disassociate themselves from them as well.'

'Well I resign from being a Personality Girl right now.'

'So do I,' says Kate.

'So do, I mean I quit as well,' says Mike.

'I wouldn't advise it,' says old meat face, 'because if you do you will be unemployed in America without visible means of support and a sponsor, and you will certainly be deported right away.'

There doesn't seem to be anything we can do. There isn't. As we board the plane again, I can't help thinking about Jake's remarks about prison pallor. I begin to weep, quietly I hope, in the back of the plane.

Poor Jake. They say he'll get two years this time.